Praise for *TETCHED*

"Thaddeus Rutkowski is one of the most original writers in America today. Once you've read his low-key, continually surprising fiction, the world will look different to you—maybe just for an hour, maybe forever."
–Alison Lurie

"No safe words inhabit this disarming yet alluring novel of emotional fractures. Thaddeus Rutkowski has written a disquieting study of estrangement—a young man's detached examination of his complex scar-tissue world. Raw, intense, and unapologetically shocking, *Tetched* is, by journey's end, an odd and inventive work of exceptional beauty."
–Rigoberto González, author of *So Often the Pitcher Goes to Water Until It Breaks*

"Thaddeus Rutkowski was 'edgy' before it became a calling card for New York City (and other) scenesters to use. Thad is the real thing—he writes directly and bravely about his personal Heart of Darkness, his adventures within and without. He writes with wit, poignancy, irony, sensuality, spareness and style. He's a true original, and an amazing performer of his work."
–Janice Eidus, author of *The Celibacy Club*

"What Thaddeus Rutkowski shares with the reader comes from a country not far from the land of Mary Gaitskill, yet his voice is like none other. It's a man's voice, both profound and crazed, arising from beginnings so brutal they make a razor strap seem easy to endure. And I thought David Sedaris was a master of black comedy!"
–June Akers Seese, author of *James Mason and the Walk-in Closet*

D1606549

TETCHED

A Novel in Fractals

by
Thaddeus Rutkowski

Behler™
PUBLICATIONS
California

Behler Publications
California

Tetched: A Novel in Fractals
A Behler Publications Book

Copyright © 2005 by Thaddeus Rutkowski
Author photograph by Randi Hoffman
Cover artwork: *Exorcising the Demons,* by Robert Carioscia
Cover design by Sun Son – www.sunsondesigns.com

All rights reserved. No part of this book may be reproduced or transmitted in any form or by any means, electronic or mechanical, including photocopying, recording, or by any information storage and retrieval system, without the written permission of the publisher, except where permitted by law.

This is a work of fiction. Names, characters, places, and incidents either are the product of the author's imagination or are used fictitiously. Any resemblance to actual persons, living or dead, events, or locales is entirely coincidental.

Library of Congress Cataloging-in-Publication Data is available
Control Number: 2004195457

FIRST EDITION

ISBN 1-933016-16-7
Published by Behler Publications, LLC
Lake Forest, California
www.behlerpublications.com

Manufactured in the United States of America

tetched \ˈtecht\ *adj* (1921): somewhat unbalanced mentally; touched [Alteration (influenced by obsolete tached, of a given disposition) of touched]

For Randi Hoffman and Shay Rutkowski

I would like to thank the editors of the following publications, where parts of this book first appeared:

Journals: *American Letters & Commentary, Asian Pacific American Journal, Barkeater: The Adirondack Review, Beet, BigCityLit.com, Blue Food, Bkyn.com, Chain, The Citizen, Curious Rooms, Epiphany, Fiction, Flyway, Front Range Review, Hayden's Ferry Review, Land-Grant College Review, Long Shot, O!!Zone, Paramour, Phantasmagoria, Phase: A Journal of Pennsylvania Writing, Rive Gauche, Salt River Review, 2ndAvenuePoetry, Spinning Jenny, Small Spiral Notebook,* and *Yama.*

Anthology: *Sweet Jesus: Poems About the Ultimate Icon* (Anthology Editions).

I also would like to thank the Corporation of Yaddo, the Dorset Colony, Kalani Oceanside Retreat, the Virginia Center for the Creative Arts, and The Writers Room for granting fellowships for this work.

CONTENTS

BELIEF SYSTEM

I believed that when I saw trees shake, I was seeing the force that made the wind blow, and that when the trees swayed faster, they pushed the air harder.

I believed that, with a piece of string, a dry chicken bone and an open range, I could be a cowboy with my own personal horse.

I believed that I was immune to electrical current, natural gas and solar rays, so I spent hours at outlets, at the stove and in the sun.

I believed that when I saw people shot on television, I was witnessing actual killing, and the actors must have been paid a lot to die.

I believed that I could parachute from a shed roof to earth, using only a cloth napkin held by its four corners to slow my fall.

I believed that I had to imitate my father and be different from my mother, because my father looked like the people around me and my mother came from a different tribe.

I believed that when my mother told me about children chasing, cornering and killing a red fox in the place where she grew up, she was trying to tell me what *not* to do.

I believed, when my father told me never to say, "Holy cow!" that I could avoid his wrath by saying, "Holy cats!" instead.

I believed that I would never learn how the other half lived through church services or Sunday school.

I believed that it would be tragic for my father to be executed for assassinating a political leader, his close friends or his immediate family, even though he often said he had to do so.

I believed that I had to choose between my parents, that I had to decide who was my favorite, in case one upped and left.

I believed that I should not ask for things, because invariably I would not get what I asked for.

I believed that if my penis turned out to be comparatively small, I could compensate by letting my hair grow long.

I believed that if my hair were long enough, I could hide behind my fringe and speak very little, if at all.

I believed that I was not tall enough to function normally in my given society, but that if I moved to Nepal, I could play on a basketball team.

I believed, when I was stoned on dope, that there was nothing more interesting than the concept of arm, save, of course, for the concept of leg.

I believed that I should refrain from heavy petting, because my sex cells were so potent they could travel through denim.

I believed that if anyone was making someone else's life hell, *I* was not the one doing it.

I believed that I could enter a place that was warm, safe and suited to the reptilian part of my brain through self-suspension, self-flagellation and self-deprecation.

I believed that I could get along best with someone who had been assaulted as a child, but that, if I couldn't find someone who had been, I would just have to go out and assault someone.

I believed that I could live with someone who did not sympathize with my obsessions, as long as I loved that person deeply enough, but I was totally wrong.

*

MOMENTUM

My father set up a still life with a vase and fruit, gave me pastels and paper, and told me to draw. I looked at the arrangement and went to work. Soon, I had a vague image on paper, and I was covered with pigment dust.

My father took my drawing, pinned it to a wall, and sprayed it with fixative. Then he opened a drawer and brought out a drawing he had made. "It's an ad for a car," he said.

The sketch showed a small automobile with a domed roof and curved fenders—a common German model. Behind the wheel was a man with a square mustache the width of his nose. The headline read: "The Hitler Bug."

"In an ad," my father explained, "you want to get people's attention. You want to appeal to their desire for world domination."

*

My father took me to visit a friend of his. When we arrived, the friend was in his garage, reassembling a car engine. His hands were covered with grease, and when he saw us he washed them in a bucket of black liquid.

My father took a bottle of beer from the man and lit a cigarette.

"You're smoking," the man said. "This bucket is filled with gasoline."

"You can put out a cigarette in gasoline," my father said, "if you're fast enough."

"Go ahead," the man said, "but you might get a close shave."

The man turned to me and held out a wire cable with a switch at its end. "Hold this," he said, "and push the button when I tell you."

He slid into the driver's seat. "Now," he said.

I squeezed my thumb, and the engine began to churn. I held the button while the man pumped the accelerator. After a minute or so, the engine exploded to life.

"Get in," the man said.

He took the car to its limit, up over a hill and down the other side. He didn't stop until we heard clanging and saw smoke coming from under the hood. "That would be a connecting rod," he told me, "blowing through the engine block."

*

My mother tried to teach me some words of her language. She pointed at my nose and said, "*Bizi.*" She touched my nose and said, "*Da bizi.*" She laughed and said, "That means 'big nose.' You have a big nose, like your father, like a Westerner."

She taught me the words for "younger sister" and "younger brother": *meimei* and *didi*. "*Meimei, didi, da bizi,*" my mother said. "*Nimen da bizi.* All of you have big noses."

*

I wanted to communicate with my brother and sister, but I was upstairs and they were downstairs, so I sent them a message through a hole in the bathroom floor. The opening had been made for a smoke duct from a stove. As I prepared to lower my note on a string, I could see the two of them sitting on a sofa, watching television.

"Why are you so idiomatic?" I wrote.

"Because we are idioms!" they wrote back.

When I got tired of passing notes, I shifted my head and looked down through the floor hole at the television screen. I saw a desert scene in a Western show: A man and a woman were buried up to their necks in sand. Ants were swarming toward their faces. I could tell that the couple would shortly be nibbled to death.

*

My mother cornered me in the bathroom. "I want to talk to you about urine," she said.

I started to leave, but she pulled me back. "It won't hurt you," she said. "It's antiseptic."

I waited without speaking.

"Taste it!" she said. "It has no nutrition, but it has no germs. This is Eastern urology."

She left me alone to test her theory. I hesitated a moment, then put a drop on my finger and put my finger to my tongue. My mother was right; it wasn't bad, but it wasn't good, either. I just had no taste for pee.

*

At night, my father didn't come home. Instead, he called my mother on the telephone.

"I'm going to meet him at the hospital," my mother told my siblings and me.

When she got back a couple of hours later, she said, "He was following his friend in his car. They were racing up a mountain, and he hit a tree."

"Who?" we asked.

"*He* did," my mother said.

When my father returned the next morning, he had a bandage on his chin. "My tooth broke off," he said, "and went through my lip. I felt fine, until I went into shock."

*

My father took me in a borrowed car to the scene of his accident. He drove up a narrow road that had a thin coating of snow, and he stopped at a curve. "Here's where the wheel left the pavement," he said. "When there was no weight on the tire, it caved in."

I saw grooves in the gravel that went in one direction, then black marks on the pavement that went the other way. My father and I followed the skid tracks into the woods and came to a broken tree. Its trunk lay on the ground, but its stump was still rooted. "The trunk came through the windshield," my father said, "but on the passenger side. That's why I didn't lose my head.

"If I didn't have you to take care of," he continued, "this wouldn't have happened. I would have had time to think."

*

At home, I walked outside by myself. Rain had fallen on snow, and the water had frozen hard. When I discovered the crust of ice, I decided to build an igloo.

I wanted to construct a dome high enough to stand under. I wanted to have a fire for cooking in the middle of the floor. I wanted to leave a hole for smoke to escape through, at the apex of the roof.

But the ice was thin, and the slabs I chopped with my hands were the size of pizza slices. I stacked the chunks in rings, piling them one on the other, around and in, until the ring rose and closed on itself. Then I built a tunnel to use as a door.

The igloo turned out to be so small that I had to crawl on my stomach to get in. Once inside, I could sit, but only with my knees pulled up to my chest.

There was no room for a fire on the floor, so I set a candle in a niche in the wall. I lit the candle and held my wet gloves next to its flame. The candle did nothing to dry the fabric, but when I brought the gloves too close, the flame singed the wool.

*

At night, I heard my father say to my mother, "You should take them somewhere. That would be better for you and for me."

"We have nowhere to go," my mother said. "Plus, if I'm not here, who would support you?"

*

In bed, I imagined that I was lying between two snow-covered hills. Clumps of snow were rolling down, gathering momentum, and crashing in the gap between.

I could control the snowballs with my hands. I could determine when they started rolling and stop them before they made contact. But as the objects got bigger and more numerous, I lost control. The cascade went beyond my reach and became an avalanche. The flood of snow grew beyond the perimeter of my room, crashed through the walls of the house, and passed the limits of the town.

Throughout the night, the creak and roar of snow filled my head.

*

DOG'S LIFE

I found the dog in the yard, in the patch of weeds between the front of the house and the street. The animal was easy to spot, because it wasn't hiding. It was on its feet and breathing, but one of its sides was crusted with blood.

I told my father about the dog, and he brought the animal inside. He told me it had been hit by shot pellets, but the wound wouldn't require treatment.

I thought the dog looked pretty good. Its eyes were clear and its short-haired coat lay flat.

*

My mother wasn't happy with the dog's arrival. "We didn't have dogs as pets where I grew up," she said. "There were dogs, but they were like pigs and chickens. They lived around people, but they didn't live indoors."

*

I walked the dog once, around the edges of the neighboring yards. The dog accepted a leash, but waited a long time before it became comfortable enough to defecate in my grasp. After that, I stopped walking the dog.

*

The dog's room was the kitchen. The animal also roamed the rest of the downstairs. It didn't come upstairs, where my family slept, because a closed door at the foot of the steps barred the way. Also, the dog knew that if it came up, my brother and I might do mean things to it. We might pull its ears or tail, or tie its paws together.

*

One morning, I walked into the kitchen and saw the dog. It was sitting under the table, hanging its head. I walked across the

room, took something from the refrigerator, sat at the table and
smelled something fecal. I scanned the room until I saw a mass of
dog droppings on the floor. I understood, then, why the animal had
a hangdog look.

*

My father decided to teach the dog to hunt. The dog was
mainly a beagle, after all. "Most hunting dogs live outside," my
father told me. "But we've been keeping this dog indoors. Its
instincts are probably gone."

My father gave the dog and me a ride to the edge of some
woods, then let us out of the car. The animal ran into the trees and
quickly vanished. My father and I picked up our guns and walked
in the direction the dog had taken. Presently, we heard a high-
pitched yipping; then we heard branches breaking and leaves
crackling. We saw a deer running toward us, with the dog in
pursuit.

"This is supposed to be a rabbit dog," my father said.

We trudged out of the woods into a field, and the dog walked
a short distance ahead of us. Presently, a rabbit thumped out of the
grass, and we saw its white tail bouncing away. I didn't react
quickly enough to shoot, but my father squeezed off a blast from
his hip.

The explosion of the 12-gauge shocked both the dog and me.
I didn't say anything; I just walked away from my father. The dog
followed behind me.

The next time my father shot at something, the dog
disappeared. When we got back to the car, we found the hunting
animal waiting for us. The dog seemed eager to get in and ride.

*

One of my father's drinking companions came to visit, and
noticed we had a dog. "That dog is living the life of Riley," the
man said. "He never had it so good. He doesn't know how good
he has it."

I looked at the dog sleeping on the kitchen linoleum, with its
back resting against the porch door. I guessed the animal was
comfortable.

"I got a dog recently," the man continued, "for my kids. It was a small, brown mongrel. But we couldn't teach it to go to the bathroom outside, so I had to get rid of it."

"How did you do that?" my father asked.

"I took it to a field and plugged it with a .22."

*

At one point, I noticed that the dog was missing. I asked the rest of my family if they were concerned about the pet's whereabouts, and my mother said, "Maybe it went out on the highway."

On the two-lane roadway, which lay a couple of hundred yards from our house, vehicles traveled at high speeds. Over the years, I had seen the corpses of cats, dogs, deer and opossums on the gravel shoulders.

After a couple of days, I believed the animal would never return.

One afternoon, as I was walking past the woodshed behind the house, I happened to look up. The dog was standing at a square hole on the second floor, looking back at me. Its lips were pulled back over its teeth, and its ears were sticking out from its triangular head. It looked like it was smiling and listening.

I guessed that the animal had gone into the shed and gotten trapped. Apparently, it had been living there, not eating or drinking, not making a sound. I called to it, and it grinned back at me, as if it were insanely happy.

*

One evening, the dog followed me to the schoolyard. I was hoping it would find a rabbit and give chase. On the mown lawn, rabbits were easy to spot, and I saw one before the dog did. I pointed out the prey and gave the dog a push with my hands. The dog saw the game and took off. The rabbit led the dog away from the school grounds toward a farmhouse.

I heard a gunshot and went to see what had happened. I found the dog standing and breathing. I couldn't tell if it had been hit; I didn't see blood. But the animal didn't want to move.

I found that I could lift the dog by curling my arms under its stomach. Carrying it like a load of wood, I walked home.

*

When I told my mother that I was concerned about the animal's well-being, she said, "I might have been a dog. My soul may have come from an animal, or from another person. Who knows where my soul will go when I die? You are the same. And so is that darned dog."

I invited the pet upstairs for the night. I tried to tell it I would not be cruel. The animal ascended the steps reluctantly.

*

MAKING CONTACT

On a clear day in the summer, I got up early. My father and siblings were still sleeping, but my mother was in her white uniform, getting ready to leave for work.

When she asked what I was going to do for the day, I said I was going fishing.

"We didn't fish when I was a child," she said. "But our city had a pond, where people thought a dragon lived. Boys would dive into the water and take messages to the bottom. Some of the boys angered the dragon and drowned."

*

Before I went to the stream, I needed to collect bait.

The ground was too dry to dig for worms, so I brought out my worm shocker—a metal curtain rod with a lamp cord attached. I pushed the rod down through the lawn as far as it would go, carried the plug into the house, and stuck the prongs into a wall outlet.

Only one strand of the double-sided cord was spliced to the rod, so there was a fifty-fifty chance that electricity was reaching the earth.

To find out if I had a live connection, I laid my hand on the grass next to the rod. I felt a slight tingling, but I couldn't tell if it was just the roughness of leaves. So I poked a finger into the soil. The cool dirt sent a buzz up through my hand and into my arm, and I knew that juice was flowing for worms.

After a few minutes, a couple of slick night crawlers lay in the sun. I put them in a plastic box, unplugged the shocker, gathered my tackle, and hiked to the creek.

*

Later, I saw my brother and sister walking toward me along the stream bank.

"We came to find you," my sister said.

"How is our father?" I asked.

"At first, he was sleeping, but now he's angry."

"Is he really angry," I asked, "or just a little angry?"

"Medium angry."

"Why?"

"We were making noise," my sister said.

"He called me a braying bastard," my brother said.

The two of them didn't have fishing rods, so I reeled in my line and walked home with them.

*

My father was in his studio with his door shut, so I went out to visit my neighbor.

The boy took me to his garage. Inside, we sat on folding chairs on a cement floor.

"I'll show you something I made in shop class," the boy said. He brought out a small board with two coils of wire and a battery mounted on it. The coils had leads that went to two metal rods. "Hold these in your hands," he said, giving me the rods.

The metal objects were lightweight and fit comfortably in my palms.

The boy touched a battery terminal with a bare wire, and a wave of oscillation went into my arms and across my chest.

I jumped from my seat. "What's this called?" I asked.

"It started as a door buzzer. Now, it's a people shocker. If you bounce up and down, it's easier to take."

I jiggled in my seat as the boy delivered more current.

*

I took a walk to the schoolyard and saw my brother on the empty playing field. He was holding a football.

"Let's run toward each other," I said. "You carry the ball, and I'll tackle you."

He shook his head. "You don't want to do that," he said.

"Yes, I do," I said.

We paced away from each other, then turned and charged.

I made a beeline for my brother, with my arms pumping and my hands clenched like claws. He ran straight toward me, without swerving or making any evasive moves. Shortly before contact, I lunged. He stepped to the side and ran around me as I hit the ground.

"Let's trade places," I said.

"Not a good idea," my brother said.

I took the football from him, walked away, clamped the ball in a flexed arm, and sprinted.

He didn't run; he just stood in my way. When my knee met his leg, I flipped to the ground. I lay there, unable to move.

"What is it?" he asked. "Is it your breadbasket?"

"No," I gasped.

After a few minutes, I got up and limped away.

*

Later, my mother told me a story.

"When I was a child," she said, "my brother and I were playing a game, like hide-and-seek. Our house had a dirt floor— most houses in southern China had dirt floors—but our living room had curtains.

"I saw the shape of my brother behind a curtain, but he couldn't see me, so I hit him. I heard him cry out and realized I'd hit him in the eye. His eye swelled and oozed and didn't heal for a long time.

"Confucius says, 'Don't blame anyone.' And you shouldn't."

*

In the evening, a friend of my father's came to visit. The man had long hair and a beard.

After a few beers, my father invited his friend and me to his studio. The three of us stood in front of a painting and looked at it. The image was of a nude man, standing sideways, with a small erection.

"There's a revolution coming," my father said. "When it gets here, I'll be ready."

"Remember what happened to Che," his friend said.

"I don't care about trends," my father said. "I just want to have enough ammunition when the shooting starts."

My father's friend picked up a ukulele that belonged to me and my siblings and started to strum it. "Some people have something to show," he said. "Those people should show what they've got."

I left the studio and went to bed.

*

The next day, I borrowed my father's home-movie camera and brought my brother and sister to an empty area next to the town's firehouse. The clearing would be the site of a carnival at the end of the summer.

I positioned my siblings in front of the skeleton of a Ferris wheel and gave them bedsheets and cardboard masks to wear. One mask was triangular, with fierce, black-outlined eyes. The other was spherical, with slanted eyes and horns.

"Kneel on the ground," I said, "and turn your heads toward me and away, toward me and away."

They followed my directions, swiveling their heads and fixing their painted eyes on me. I crouched and moved, catching their pantomime from different angles.

Next, I walked through the town by myself, focusing on houses and clicking the film forward one frame at a time. I wanted the effect of animated architecture.

When I got home, the family dog was in the yard. I walked toward the animal, and it sniffed at my camera. I filmed its nose swinging up toward the lens.

*

PRACTICE SESSIONS

My father called me to his workroom.

I stood in the doorway while he sat at his drafting table.

"I don't want you to be a sissy," he said.

"I had a mean sergeant in the Army," he continued. "Once, he made everyone do push-ups with him. He stood at the front of the troop, and all of the men got down on the ground. Then the sergeant dropped and started pumping. One by one, the men collapsed, but the sergeant kept going. Finally, I was the only one left doing push-ups with him.

"Now, it's your turn," my father said to me. "Get down and give me twenty!"

I knelt, then extended my body. I flexed my elbows and touched my chin to the floor.

*

In phys. ed. class at school, I heard the coach call out, "Mouse!"

At first, I didn't know who he was talking to. Then I realized that I fit the description, so I walked furtively to the front of the gym.

"Jump!" he said.

I crouched at a line painted on the floor. I swung my arms and leaped. The coach marked where my heels landed.

"Six feet, three inches," he said. "Again!"

I went back to the line, concentrated all of my potential energy into my leg muscles, and sprang forward.

"Six feet, three-and-a-half inches," he said.

He pointed to a thick cord hanging from the ceiling. "Now, the jungle rope!"

I grabbed the stiff hemp, clenched my knees around it, and went up it like a cat.

*

At home, my father sent me out to buy cigarettes. I walked down the street to the post office/general store and asked the postmistress for a package of nonfilters. She looked over the counter at me and said, "You're not old enough to buy cigarettes."

I walked back up the street and went into the hotel bar. I dropped coins into the cigarette machine and levered a pack into the tray.

*

In the house, my father was sitting at the kitchen table with his head propped on his hands. I gave him the cigarettes, and he slapped the pack against his palm, then slit the cellophane.

"I'm not Picasso," he said as he lit up. "But I don't have to be. I'm going to sell art prints for five dollars apiece. I don't care about the *nouveaux riches*. My art is for the masses.

"Just wait and see," he added. "Twenty years from now, you won't believe where I've been."

*

I sat for a photo portrait at school.

Soon afterward, I received a paper sheet of wallet-sized prints. When I studied the proofs, I saw that I looked a lot like my mother, and not at all like the rest of my classmates.

With scissors, I cut the pictures apart and stored them in a drawer.

One day, I asked a girl if she would trade pictures with me. She said yes and gave me her photo in an envelope. Later, when I opened the package, I saw that the photo was not of her, but of another girl in the school.

*

My father woke me in the dark.

I put on layers of clothing, then helped him load fishing tackle into his car.

He drove for a few miles and parked on a dirt pull-off. Through the car window, I could see white riffles and hear the rush of water.

I took off my shoes and put on hip boots, then twisted my rod together at its ferrules. I threaded fly line through the ringlets, tied on a leader and hook, and crimped a lead weight around the leader with my teeth.

I waded into the riffles and waited for the sky to brighten.

When I felt a strike, I started jumping up and down.

"Don't act like a jackanapes!" my father said.

I released the tension on the line and felt the fish break free.

*

On the way home, my father stopped at a bar. He led me inside, and we sat at a Formica-topped table. I had a soft drink, while he had a bourbon and a beer.

When we got back into the car, he said, "I'm going to take this boat places."

He sat for a long time with his head against the steering wheel. Then he turned the key, raced the engine and shot out of his parking space.

*

I noticed that my throat was hurting, so I told my mother about it. She picked up a flashlight and said, "Open your mouth."

I relaxed my jaw, and she pressed a flat stick against my tongue.

"Ew!" she said. "Your tonsils are swollen, and they're covered with white spots."

She opened her mouth and turned toward the light. "Look at my throat," she said.

I took the flashlight and looked in.

"I had my tonsils out when I was a child," she said. "In China, it was a serious operation. My parents had to take care of me for a long time. They fed me tofu. Now, my throat tissue is flat."

She poked a cotton-tipped toothpick against the back of my throat. When I choked, she pulled the toothpick out. "I'll put this in a culture dish at the hospital lab," she said. "When I'm not busy, I'll check to see how it blooms."

*

A boy who lived nearby took me fishing. When we got to the creek, he pointed to trout where they lay, camouflaged against the sand.

He dropped in his bait and almost immediately hooked a fish. After he lifted it onto the bank, he said, "You have to whack it out."

He grabbed the fish by its middle and hammered its head against a stone. The fish quivered, then stopped moving.

"Let's go fishing again tomorrow," the boy said.

The next morning, I put on my hip boots, picked up my gear and walked to the boy's house. When I knocked on the door, his mother answered.

"We're supposed to go fishing," I said.

"He's not home," she told me.

*

At home, I lay down on my bed. It was midday, so I pulled the shades. I didn't fall asleep, but I didn't have the energy to move.

I fantasized about capturing the girl who had switched photos on me. I would build rooms underground, on the side of the nearby mountain. The ceiling would be made of glass, and she would live there, under the glass.

Sometimes I would fasten her to a table, exposed to the sun. I would stay in a separate room and watch her through a one-way mirror. When I came to where she was, I would hide my face behind a mask.

*

When my father saw me, he told me to get up. I heard his voice but didn't respond. When he yelled, "Fall out, Sweet Pea!" I rose from the bed.

He told me to take my brother and sister for a walk. Before we left, he gave us butterfly nets and a killing jar.

The three of us walked along a lane toward a fallow farm. At one spot, a large dog charged at us, and we ran.

We came to a pond and saw some sulfur-colored butterflies clustering above the mud bank, but we didn't use our nets. Instead, we kept walking.

The track we were on went up over a ridge, across a basin, to the tree line of the nearest mountain.

Holding our nets like weapons, we hiked uphill.

*

CHOOSING BETWEEN

When my father woke in the morning and saw that the television was on, he said to my siblings and me, "Turn off the idiot box! Get outside and do something!"

All three of us started to leave, but my father turned to my sister and said, "Not you."

My brother and I went out to the back yard. We looked around until we saw a couple of baseball bats leaning against the house. We picked some stones from the ground, tossed them in the air, and swatted them toward the neighboring houses. The stones struck roofs and aluminum siding, but didn't hit any windows.

When our arms got tired, we looked at our father's vegetable garden. In one trench there was a row of yellow-green lettuce leaves. In a parallel groove, dark-green onion spikes stood. Next to the onions, beans were sprouting. Their cotyledons were curled where they were breaking through the ground.

"I want to show you something," my brother said.

He led me to the outhouse, which my father had made into a toolshed. My brother opened the door and pointed to a motor-driven plow. The machine had handles, but instead of wheels it had rotary blades.

My brother dragged the contraption outside and pulled the starter cord, and the engine came to life. He guided the machine across the garden as the blades churned through the soil.

"It's a man-killer," he said.

*

When we went back into the house, we found our sister watching television. Our father was not around.

"Where is he?" I asked.

"He went back to bed," she said.

"What were you doing?" I asked.

"Listening to him talk," my sister said.

"Was he upset?" I asked.

"No," she said. "He made breakfast for me. Then he got tired."

*

I walked alone to the schoolyard. The playing fields were empty, and the school building was dark. I tested an outdoor fountain by twisting the valve sprocket, but no water came out.

I walked around the building until I came to a parking lot. A couple dozen majorettes were practicing routines on the paved area. They were wearing sweaters, skirts, high socks and saddle shoes. They stepped in unison, twirling batons. Sometimes they threw the batons into the air and caught the flashing sticks as they spun downward. Occasionally, the twirlers missed, and their batons bounced on the ground.

I wanted to be a drum major. I wanted to wear a top hat and carry a brass staff as I led the corps.

I spotted an umbrella in a trash can. I hooked the umbrella over my forearm and fell into step beside the majorettes. I held the accessory like a cane and tapped its tip on the pavement as I walked.

The lead majorette said to me, "Go home, little boy."

"I'm not a little boy," I said. "I'm a young man with an umbrella."

*

At home, I walked quietly past my father's workroom so as not to disturb him, but he saw me and called me in. He pointed at a sheet of paper with calligraphy on it and asked, "What's that?"

I saw a couple of small red spots on the paper. "Is it ink?" I asked.

"It's blood," he said. "I was blowing on the page when I noticed I was spitting blood. I don't know where it's coming from."

To show me, he huffed at the paper, and more red droplets soaked into the sheet.

*

At school, I had to run the 800 in gym class. Before the race began, the coach divided the runners into two teams: the Shirts and the Skins. Unfortunately, I was assigned to the Skins, and so I had to take off my T-shirt. Bare-torsoed, I followed my herd for a quarter-mile around an oval-shaped track. Soon, my group moved out ahead of me. When I finished, I had to bend over and put my hands on my knees so I could breathe.

When I got back inside the school, one of the girls I had seen practicing her majorette moves said to me, "I saw you running out there. You were shirtless. You looked skinny, but wiry."

*

Later, my father had surgery. When he came home from the hospital, he said, "They used a hammer and a chisel on my jaw. When I woke up, I didn't know where I was. So I told the nurses where to go. I don't care what they thought. They don't know what I'm about."

A few days later, I heard my father yelling during the night. "The surgeons didn't know what they were doing," he said. "They left something in."

"You didn't take of yourself," my mother said to him. "You were supposed to clean your mouth so you wouldn't get an infection."

"I have no time for that," my father said.

"This is what happens then," my mother said.

My father kept my family awake all night with his shouting.

*

In school, I went to a play rehearsal. I had been cast as a Greek soldier named Haemon. At one point I had to embrace a Greek noblewoman who was bigger than I was. I put my arms around her waist, stood on my toes, and brought my face to hers, but I couldn't kiss her.

The director said to me, "Come on. Your name's Haemon, but you act like Pocahontas."

The student playing a Greek king said to me, "That was the most embarrassing kiss I've ever seen."

I wanted to clasp Antigone with authority. I wanted to wrap my elbows around her neck and give her a lip smack. But the next time I went in for the smooch, all I could manage was a peck.

Soon after that, another student replaced me in the role of Haemon.

*

At home, my father said to me, "You have a choice. You can wring your hands and become a fairy. Or you can do what I did. I found an Asian woman."

When I didn't say anything, my father said, "You're dismissed."

*

I went out to the toolshed and brought out the man-killer. I pulled the starter cord and gripped the handles tightly. The machine dragged me forward as it chewed into the ground.

I enlarged my father's vegetable garden. I guided the plow around the perimeter and watched the motor-driven blades grind through the lawn grass.

*

Inside, I took a hardcover book off my father's shelf and pulled an old letter from between the pages. The letter was from my father's father. In it, he gave my father some advice about his upcoming wedding. "Your mother and I were glad to meet your fiancée," the letter read. "You both seem to love each other. But we can't encourage you to go ahead with your plans. The marriage might be fine for you and your wife. But think of your children. They won't belong with Asians, and they won't belong with other people, either. Would that be fair to them?"

*

I climbed a ladder, opened a trapdoor, and stepped into the attic. The warm, still air smelled of dust. Near an air vent, wasps buzzed around a papery nest. I lay down on the wood floor, which was unfinished and splintery. I spread out my arms and legs. After a while, I could feel my skin sweating. If I stayed this way long enough, I figured, I would die of thirst.

I stayed there for as long as I could, until the sun apparently moved and the heat faded. I climbed down the ladder and closed the trapdoor, so that no one would know where I had been.

*

TIGHT CIRCLES

On a hot day, my father rounded up my brother and sister and me and took us for a walk. My siblings and I carried butterfly nets, while our father carried a rifle.

The three of us saw no flashy specimens—no pipevine swallowtails or regal fritillaries—so we had no reason to run across the fields with our nets pumping. Instead, we moved slowly. Sometimes, we let our nets drag on the ground.

When we came to a mud hole, we spotted a snake coiled on the ground. Its skin was metallic brown, with a light-and-dark saddle pattern.

"It has a triangular head," my father said. "It looks like a copperhead."

He picked up a stick and approached the snake, but the reptile didn't slide away. Instead, it struck at the stick, slinging its head forward and showing its mouth's white lining.

My father shouldered his rifle and fired. The snake jerked, then went still. My father draped the carcass over his stick and, holding the assemblage of snake and branch like a divining rod, carried the dead reptile home.

In his studio, he compared the snake to photographs in a guidebook. "It was a water snake," he announced. "It was harmless."

*

I sat on the couch and looked at our aquarium, which sat on a cabinet next to a windowsill. Not much light came through the window, because there was a porch roof right outside. The water level in the tank, I noticed, was about two inches.

Three guppies, all female, swam among plants my father had collected from the nearby creek. The tufted vines crowded the water.

I picked up a small can of fish food and shook it over the water. The guppies rose and kissed the surface with their tiny, round mouths.

*

My father wasn't present for supper, so I sat with my brother and sister at the kitchen table while our mother stood and watched us.

"You have to finish all of your food," she said. "When I was a child, we had to eat all of our rice. We didn't eat like people here, with dishes on the table. We held our bowls to our chins and shoveled the rice with our chopsticks. We couldn't leave a single grain. Each leftover piece of rice was a seed of bad luck."

I looked at the food on my plate. I had no rice and no chopsticks. Even so, I decided to pick every particle from the ceramic.

*

At school, I arrived at the cafeteria late for lunch, so I stood at the back of the food line. I noticed that the person ahead of me was a girl with cooties, or so I'd been told. I'd never seen a cootie, but I understood that an infestation of the things was something to avoid.

I sneaked up a few places in line, but a cafeteria monitor saw me. He locked an elbow around my neck and began to sand my scalp with the knuckles of his free hand. "Why did you cut in line?" he asked.

"I didn't want to get cooties," I said.

"That takes the cake," he said. He kept my neck clamped in his bent arm until he finished grinding my head; then he sent me to the back of the line.

After I'd gotten my lunch tray, I saw there was only one empty seat in the room. I sat next to the girl with cooties and ate along with her.

*

I went to the school auditorium for a study period. There was no teacher or proctor, so several students were sitting on the stage apron. I found a seat in the audience area.

One of the boys on the stage brought out a pair of handcuffs and passed them around.

"Where did you get them?" someone asked.

"From my father," the boy said. "He's a cop."

One of the girls said, "Put them on me."

"Why?" the boy asked.

"I want to see how they feel."

She held out her hands, and the boy clicked the rings shut. She pulled against the metal to find out how far her wrists would go.

The boy looked at the rest of us and gestured toward the girl. "Who's first?" he asked.

"First for what?" someone asked.

*

In the evening, a boy came to visit me.

We started to play chess in my bedroom, but after a while the boy said that he wanted to play doctor.

He told me to lie on my stomach. After I did, he pulled down my pants. He took a cork from my chemistry set and pushed the narrow end between my buttocks. "We'll see if you pass the exam," he said.

Next, he told me to lie on my back. Using his thumb and forefinger like forceps, he grasped my penis. "I'm going to show you something that feels good," he said.

He moved his hand like a piston while kneading and pinching my penile skin. My outstretched shaft lengthened and darkened, and the tip started to twitch. My primary care physician varied his angle of motion and bore down on the marrow of my boner. "Come on," he commanded. "Squirt!"

But my jumping bonal tip stayed dry.

*

After the boy left, my father asked what we had been doing.

"Playing chess," I said, "practicing the Nimzo-Indian defense."

My father called to my mother, and she came running.

"What happened?" she asked.

"They were jacking off!" he said.

"Well, what did you do when you were a child?" my mother asked.

"I didn't close my door!" my father said.

*

I went out to the cement porch and rode my bicycle in circles. It was a small area and a big bike, so I had to ride carefully. I cut the front wheel sharply each time I approached a wall.

My father and a friend of his were sitting inside, drinking beer and smoking cigarettes. I could see them through the screen door.

"I'm going to pull my children out of school," my father said.

"You should send them to church," his friend said, "so they can see how the other half lives."

"My wife is a Confucian," my father said, "and I was excommunicated."

I heard a loud sound on the street. I looked and saw that my father's friend's car had coasted from its parking spot and crashed through a neighbor's porch railing. The chassis was resting on a pile of splintered wood.

*

After the friend had retrieved his car and settled with the neighbors, he came over to me. "Do me a favor," he said. "The next time you go out, take some rubbers with you."

He reached into his wallet and handed me a silvery, airtight packet. I pocketed the sexware for later examination.

*

On a Sunday morning, I saw a line of cars heading for the church down the street. As the cars proceeded, I could hear tower bells chiming a hymn.

I got on my bicycle and rode to the white-sided building. As I approached the entrance, I saw a billboard with the quote of the day: "To bear the cross cheerfully is the secret of the saints."

Everyone in town, except for my family, seemed to be inside the building. Cars filled the parking lot and lined both sides of the street.

A couple of hours later, as I rode my bike in circles, I heard the bells ringing again and saw the same cars driving away, in the opposite direction.

*

MISFIRES

My father brought me with him for a walk, and we ended up at the hotel bar. Inside, a few grizzled men were sitting on stools. The only light came from a television screen.

"There's a guy hitchhiking at the edge of town," one of the men said. "A black guy."

"He'd better not be there long," another said.

"If he's there when I drive by," said another, "he'll become a janitor in a drum."

My father took me home and went out again, this time in his car.

When he came back, he had the hitchhiker with him.

"He said he'd visit with us," my father said. "Later, I'll take him to the university."

The stranger crouched so that his head was on the level of mine. He held out his hand, but I didn't respond. When he didn't move away, I clasped his hand.

That night, there was a carnival at the local fire hall, and my father said that the hitchhiker should take me. "I'm going to the bar," my father said. "Maybe I'll meet you later."

The hitchhiker and I walked down the street to the floodlit grounds. As we got closer, I could smell boiling oil and fried potatoes.

We wandered on crushed grass between plywood booths, passing a paddle-wheel game, a penny pitch, a dart wall, and a hardball tunnel. When we came to the Ferris wheel, we got tickets and climbed into a bucket. At the top of our arc, we could see all of the carnival-goers, the field filled with parked cars, and the one street of the town.

No one talked to us the entire time we were at the carnival, and my father didn't show up.

*

The next morning, I went outside to catch the school bus.

While I waited, a boy called out: "Jap!" He was standing on the other side of the street with a group of his friends.

"Come here!" he yelled. "I want to pull out your esophagus and shove it down your throat!"

I stayed on my side of the street.

"I want to rip out your femur and hit you over the head with it!"

On the bus, the boy and his friends took the prime seats in the back. I sat next to the driver.

*

When I arrived at gym class, I found out that all of the boys had to stretch for wrestling. I got down on the mat with the rest of my classmates. We lay on our backs and pushed up with our feet so that our weight was on our craniums. We balanced like crabs, then pivoted on our heads so that we were face-down.

After the "bridging," we practiced Greco-Roman moves. We "sat out" in sequence, lifted each other like firefighters, then broke each other down.

Next, our coach paired us for matches. He chose as my opponent the boy who had wanted to remove my gullet and thighbone. We were both about the same size.

The boy and I dropped into the referee's position. I supported myself on my hands and knees; my antagonist held my near elbow with one hand and wrapped his free arm around my waist.

On the command of "Ready! Wrastle!" the boy on top attempted to pull my limbs out from under me. I quickly extended an arm and leg, and both of us slithered sideways. He crooked an elbow around my arm and tried to lever me onto my back. But I twisted my torso, pried his arm away and stood up. He grabbed the backs of my knees, but I planted my feet, and we staggered out of the ring.

Our struggle lasted about five minutes. When it was over, the coach declared the match a draw.

In the locker room, I sat on a bench to change. As I took off my gym clothes, I heard an athletic boy say to the boy who had wrestled with me, "For a little guy, you sure have a big dick."

I didn't want to be naked in front of the rest of the boys, so I didn't take a shower. I stuffed my T-shirt, shorts and strap into my gym bag, put on my street clothes and went to class.

*

When I got home, I had to practice my flute.

I went to my bedroom and took the instrument out of its case. I twisted the three silver parts together, brought the mouthpiece to my lips, and rolled the airhole back and forth for a comfortable embouchure. I blew gently and produced a jug-like tone. Then I blew hard and got a high whistle.

When the family dog heard my shrill sound, it started to howl. I kept making high notes, so that the dog and I performed a duet.

*

At dinner, I told my father I wanted to play in the marching band.

"You want to wear a uniform and goose-step?" my father said. "No son of mine is growing up to be cannon fodder."

He turned to my brother and sister. "None of you is to associate with Americans anymore," he said.

"What about their friends?" my mother asked.

"They will stop seeing their friends."

"But we live in America," my mother said.

"Americans are herd animals," my father said. "They march in step and worship the dollar."

"I work to support you and the children," my mother said.

"Have you heard the saying," my father asked, " 'A woman with a wagging tongue is a stairway to disaster'?"

"There's another saying," my mother said. " 'The best time to visit the wise man is when he isn't home.' "

My father stood up. "I'm going to the hotel bar," he said.

*

I heard my mother talking on the telephone in Chinese.

When she was finished, she said, "That was my brother. He heard from my father."

"Where is your father?" I asked.

"He's living in a village near the city where I grew up. He can't leave there. He has false teeth, because he was hit in work camp. Otherwise, he's healthy."

"Can you talk to him?" I asked.

"I can write to him. But I've forgotten a lot of characters, so I'll write in English."

"Can he read it?"

"Yes. That's why he disappeared."

Late at night, I was awakened by my father's voice. "He's not coming here!" he shouted. "I can't take care of you people! I'm not a nursemaid!"

*

For a birthday present, my father gave me a hunting gun: an over-and-under, with a rifle barrel on top and a shotgun barrel on the bottom. "You're old enough to hunt by yourself," he said.

Then he told me to hit the woods.

I left the house and walked on a farm lane toward a hillside.

The gun was heavy. At first, I cradled it in my arms, with one hand wrapped around the trigger guard and a thumb on the safety. This way, I could smoothly bring the stock to my shoulder, cock the hammer, aim and fire.

As I crept through a stand of trees next to a field, I kicked at brush piles, stopped, listened, then moved forward and repeated the routine. But I didn't see any game. After a mile or so, I dropped my arms and let the gun dangle. Sometimes, I carried the firearm over my shoulder, like a soldier.

After a while, I put the gun on the ground and stood motionless.

When I took my next step, I heard a drumming of wings and saw the blur of an escaping bird. I grabbed the gun, brought it to my waist, and fired blindly into the trees. The shot tore through the brush, scattering leaves and twigs.

As I fumbled to reload, I saw the bird break out of the trees and head for clear sky.

*

UNNATURAL WONDERS

My mother told me that her father was coming to visit us. She said that he'd been freed, allowed to leave his country.

For the occasion, my mother did something unusual. She made Chinese food. I watched while she powered up the electric stove—only two of the four heating elements worked—and brought out a couple of pots. She spent some time washing, chopping and measuring, then walked away. When she came back, smoke was leaking from under a pot's lid. "It's all right," she said. "The black part is on the bottom."

When my grandfather arrived, he seemed full of energy. He sat with my family at the kitchen table. "A circle of people," my mother explained, "is like the shape of the moon. When the moon is full, the family should come together."

My mother brought out a glass with green liquid in it. "This is the cooking water from the vegetables," she said.

She passed the glass around, and we all sipped the warm juice.

My father held chopsticks in one hand and a glass of yellow wine in the other. "Chiang Kai-shek had some good ideas," he said. "He was no Democrat. He provoked civil war."

I noticed that some of the rice tasted like carbon, so I tried to separate the burnt bits from the unburnt ones.

My mother said, "I remember the Moon Festival; it was on the fifteenth day of the eighth month. Families would gather outdoors, and we could hear an *er hu* playing in the distance. At the end of the day, we would eat moon cakes."

My brother and sister and I looked at our grandfather. One of us asked, "Why are you still alive?"

"I had a good attitude in work camp," he said. "Mostly, I was left alone. But once, while I was waiting in line for food, a guard hit me in the face. I turned away, even though he'd knocked out some teeth. I have a good set of false teeth now."

All of us commented on the older man's good English. "I learned it in college here," he said. "Back in China, I remembered the language."

My father gulped some wine and said, "A revolution is not a garden party. Justice grows out of the barrel of a gun."

My grandfather laughed and said, "I guess I'm not the only one lucky to be alive."

"You'd speak differently if you'd been on the Long March," my father said.

"If I were on the March," the older man said, "I'd sing a marching song."

After our meal, I looked out a window and saw a full moon. I tried to stay focused on the glowing disc until it moved, but I didn't have the patience to perceive lunar motion. All I saw were gray features on an impossibly bright surface.

*

My grandfather got ready to leave the next day. When I asked my mother why he was going so soon, she said, "Your father can't stand him anymore."

Before he departed, my grandfather gave me a scroll made of small bamboo sticks. I unwound the sheet and saw an image of a tiger surrounded by Chinese characters.

"Maybe someday," he said, "you'll be able to read the message."

*

I got on a yellow bus and rode toward school. At the front of the cabin was a sign with the headline "Bus rules." The headline had been altered with a knife blade to read, "Bust rules."

Next to me, two teenage girls were reading a paperback thriller. "Listen to this," one said. " 'I was sitting alone in my office, when a woman in high heels walked through the door. She opened her trench coat and shoved her thirty-eights in my face. And then she took out a *gun*.' "

"You mean," the other girl said, "her gun wasn't a thirty-eight?"

"No," said the first, "her gun was a forty-five! Her *chest* was a thirty-eight!"

One of the girls turned to me and said, "Cover your virgin ears!"

I flattened my hands over the sides of my head.

"You look like a monkey," she said. "But at least you'll hear no evil."

I kept my mouth shut, so I would also speak no evil.

*

During class, I tried to break pencils by wedging them between my fingers and slapping my hand against my knee. The shorter the pencils were, the harder they were to break. I didn't know if my metacarpal bones would snap before the pencil wood.

*

In the afternoon, I went to a pep rally for the football team. I watched from the bleachers while cheerleaders performed on the gym floor. For one skit, they wore Indian headdresses and danced around an imaginary campfire, waving their arms as if summoning rain. They tied a "squaw" from the opposing team to a pole and lifted the ends, then walked around with their captive hanging from the rod.

As I was leaving the rally, a teacher said to me, "I'm casting actors for a school play. You'd make a good Siamese prince. Can you wear bloomers and put glitter on your face?"

"No," I said.

"Can you put your fists on your waist and say, 'What? What? What?' "

I stood with my balled hands on my belt and my elbows out and said loudly, "What! What! What!"

*

When I told my father I would be in a school play, he said, "They just want you because you look Asian. Who are you going to be, a coolie? Will you braid your hair and wear a straw hat? No child of mine is going to play a coolie!"

*

I hiked outside to complete an assignment for biology class. My mission was to find unusual trees, then collect their leaves.

I followed a television cable wire strung along the side of a hill. At first, I walked on a dirt path, but near the top of the slope I had to climb over boulders. I went on all fours, using my toes and fingers.

At the summit, I stood on a trail that ran along the crest. I looked down and saw a bear galloping toward me. The large black animal was running like a dog, moving uphill fast. It didn't look at me as it passed.

I held onto my biology specimens—a bag full of green leaves—and watched as the bear traveled between the trunks of trees.

*

At home, my mother was talking on the telephone in Chinese and my father was in his studio, so I didn't tell anyone about the animal sighting. Instead, I called one of the cheerleaders I'd seen at the pep rally. When she found out who was calling, she put her mother on the phone.

"Do I know you?" her mother asked.

"I don't think so," I said.

"Why are you calling?" she asked.

"I got a part in a play," I said.

"What's the play about?" the woman asked. "Is it a dirty story?"

"No," I said.

"It has to be," she said. "That's all you people think about." Then she hung up.

*

I picked up my air rifle, pointed the barrel at my shoe, and pulled the trigger. The pellet stung, but it didn't go through the leather.

Next, I shot at my hand. I put my palm over the end of the barrel and fired. The pain was intense, but the pellet didn't go through my skin. It just left a blood blister.

I debated shooting my eye. I was pretty sure that if my eyelid were open, the soft part wouldn't remain intact. But if my eyelid were closed, it might offer sufficient protection. Either way, I figured, I would see no evil.

*

I unfurled the scroll my grandfather had given me. Its tiny sticks were held together with thread.

When I asked my mother to translate the characters, she said, "I think they mean, 'Coming in from fragrant rain, do not brush your hat. Bathed in sweet drops, do not shake your coat.' "

I found a hammer and nail and tacked the scroll to the wall of my bedroom.

I wanted to write a letter to my grandfather. I knew that his first name was Qi Xing or Cheer Sing, but I didn't know which to use. For a while, no words would come. Then I forced myself to make a choice.

*

LIKE THE REESE'S CUP

My father brought home a new friend of his—a teenaged boy he'd met along the highway. The boy had been hitchhiking, and my father had picked him up. The boy's name was Reese, "like the Reese's Cup," he told me.

My father wanted Reese to stay with us, so he unfolded the living-room couch and put down sheets and blankets.

I came into the room while the boy was sitting on the bed. He smelled like he hadn't bathed in days.

"Do you go to school?" I asked.

"Yes," he said, "but my first school expelled me because I tried to blow it up."

"With what?" I asked.

"Dynamite."

"Where do you go now?"

"I go to a free school. But it's not really free; it's more like a prison."

"How did you get here?" I asked.

"I escaped."

*

I took Reese for a tour around town. I led him across backyards until we came to a chicken shed. We slid the latch on the wooden door and went in.

The shed was dark inside, but we could see chickens nesting on shelves. The floor was soft, because it was covered with straw. The place smelled like ammonia. White chicken droppings coated every surface.

"Which is worse," Reese asked, "cow manure or guano?"

"I don't know," I said.

"I think guano is much worse," he said. "I'll pick up cow manure with my hands, but I won't touch bird droppings."

"I feel the same way about dog doo," I said.

Outside the chicken coop, we found a hutch with rabbits and a mesh cage containing guinea pigs. We considered the relative nastiness of those animals' excrement.

*

Reese and I watched while my father gave an informal art show. He propped a couple of paintings on the floor and stood next to them. On the canvases, archways framed images of suffering men, some of whom were hanging on crosses.

"After my opening," my father explained, "the reviewers called me a Catholic artist. They didn't mean my work was comprehensive. They meant it was catechistic. I test the viewer by posing questions. If you're on a cross, can you help but look like Christ? If you're Christ, how should people treat you?"

Later, Reese said to me, "I noticed that when your father talks, he doesn't look at me. I may as well not be there."

*

I took Reese to school with me and introduced him as an out-of-town friend.

Somehow, he had acquired a bottle of wine. He sat in the back row and drank the wine out of a paper bag. When a teacher told him that no food or drink was allowed in the classrooms, he went out to the hallway to finish the bottle.

Later, he said to me, "You and I are the ones who don't belong. We're on the edge of something. No one else even knows what it is."

*

At supper, my father said, "This country's biggest problem is compulsory education. Who passed that law? Why should children be forced to go to school? We should educate our children ourselves."

"Are you doing that?" my mother asked.

"I spend all of my time with children," my father said, "even though I have no time for children."

"There's a Chinese saying," my mother said. " 'Live to old age, study to old age. There remain three-tenths that cannot be known.' "

*

Reese and I hitchhiked to a farm that I had heard about. The place was in a neighboring valley, so we traveled for about an hour to get there. From the highway, we had to walk on a dirt road to reach the house.

Inside, we met some teenagers. There were no adults present. We sat at a large table and listened to records on an old-fashioned stereo. One of the songs was about motherless children.

There was a can of tobacco on the table, and we took turns rolling cigarettes. I didn't know how to tighten the paper, so my cigarette came out lumpy.

"It looks like a drill bit," Reese said.

"No," someone else said, "it looks like a pregnant snake."

The fumes felt like dry fire in my throat, but I smoked the cigarette down.

When we decided to leave, we realized we had no way to get home. Fortunately, an Amish shuttle—a vehicle used by the Amish but driven by someone who wasn't in the sect—picked us up.

When my father found out where we had been, he became upset. "You shouldn't have gone there," he said to me. "There's no supervision. Those kids do whatever they please. It's a queer farm. It's Boys Town."

"There were a couple of girls," I said.

"Don't talk back!" my father said. "I know the signs of pansies. They grow their hair long, like yours."

"You have a mustache," I pointed out.

"You don't know what I'm about! I'm not like the rest of these people! Do you hear me?"

"Yes," I mumbled.

As before, my father did not look at Reese as he spoke.

*

I brought Reese to my father's gun rack, and we examined the firearms. Reese picked up a .22 rifle. "Do you know how to use this?" he asked.

I worked the action and loaded the gun, then gave it to my co-conspirator. We looked out a window and saw a bird perched on an electrical wire. The bird was small, but it wasn't far away. I opened the window, and Reese pointed the barrel of the gun through the space.

At the shot, the bird fluttered away, but the power wire snapped apart. The loose strands swung down toward the ground. Simultaneously, the appliances in the house went off.

When we looked out the window, we didn't see any signs of electrical life. The entire town was dead. We decided to tell anyone who asked that we had seen lightning hit the wire.

*

At some point, Reese disappeared. I didn't know whether my father had given him a ride to the highway, or if he had left on his own. In any event, he didn't say goodbye. I knew he was gone for good when I saw that the couch mattress had been folded away.

*

When I walked past my mother, she slapped me on the chest. "Walk straight!" she said. "Don't slouch. Lift your head. Remember what Confucius said: 'The virtue of balance is highest.' "

I corrected my posture and walked away. But as soon as I was out of her sight, I hunched my shoulders and looked at the ground.

*

TRIAL RUNS

At school, I was given a science project. The idea was to determine the learning ability of a mouse.

I bought a white specimen at a pet store, brought the animal home and kept it in a wire cage on my dresser.

I built a maze out of cardboard by cutting strips for barriers and gluing them edgewise onto a base. The maze was T-shaped, and when the mouse came to the single intersection, it had to turn right or left. It would find a piece of cheese in one direction, a dead end in the other.

The mouse quickly learned the correct route. After a couple of tries, it never made a wrong turn.

*

When my father saw my maze, he decided to construct a more complicated labyrinth. His box had many paths and obstacles, and numerous changes of direction on the way to the cheese.

I tracked the mouse's progress by tracing its trails on paper. Sometimes, the animal would get partway without error, then return to its starting point. Other times, it would refuse to go past the first fork. Occasionally, it would reach the cheese, but its arrival would seem accidental. The mouse was never able to duplicate a successful run.

My diagrams of its progress looked like bundles of tangles, with no beginnings or ends.

*

When my mother saw me walking into my room, she asked, "What are you going to do in there?"

"Homework," I said.

"You have a candle in your room," she said, "People who take drugs have candles. They use them to heat drugs. Are you on drugs?"

"No," I said.

In my room, I lit a candle. I passed a finger back and forth through the flame near the wick. The flame flickered, but I didn't get burned.

I experimented by bringing my palm to the flame from above. The closest safe distance, I learned, was about four inches. I deliberately held my hand closer, in the burn zone. When I took my hand away, I saw a red disk covering the creases on my palm.

*

At night, I listened to my mouse running on its exercise wheel. The moving metal made a squeaking sound that I couldn't ignore.

When my father saw that I was awake, he came into my room. He sat on a chair and told me a story about his time in the Army.

"When I was in boot camp," he said, "a hypnotist visited our battalion. He stood on a platform and asked everyone to raise their hands.

" 'Your arms are like iron,' the hypnotist said. 'Water is rushing through them. You can't move or bend them.' "

" 'Now,' the hypnotist said, 'Put your arms down.' "

"Almost all of the soldiers dropped their arms, except for two men. The hypnotist called those men to the stage and turned them into human furniture.

"That was how I learned to put myself in a trance," my father said. "It helped me when I heard that my sister had died. I couldn't leave the post, and I couldn't sleep. That's why I started drinking and became an artist."

After my father had left my room, I imagined a waterfall inside my body. My limbs became rigid, and none of my muscles would move.

*

During the night, my mother looked into my room. I woke and saw her standing in the doorway.

"Are you wheezing?" she asked.

I inhaled, and air whistled as it entered my lungs. I exhaled and produced a similar screech.

"I don't think so," I said.

*

In the morning, I discovered that my mouse had escaped. Its cage was still locked, but two of the wire bars were bent outward.

I took a quick look around my room, eyeing the channels where the walls met the floor, searching for holes to the outside. When I didn't see the animal, I gave up the search.

*

My mother drove me to visit a doctor.

At the clinic, the doctor called me into an exam room and gave me four shots, two in each arm. Then he told me to go to another room and wait.

As I sat, the skin around the needle punctures swelled to the size of golf balls.

The doctor came to me and touched the lumps. "You are allergic to mold, pollen, smoke, dust, pet hair and your own hair," he said.

"When I turn eighteen," I said, "will you write a letter to my draft board saying I'm unable to serve?"

"No," the doctor said. "First, I need to see you seized by an asthma attack. I have to be there when you gasp for air and turn red in the face. I have to put you in the hospital and keep you there until your contortions subside. Then I can write the letter."

"I want a medical deferment," I said.

"You are fit for the jungle," the doctor said.

*

To toughen me up, my father bought me a rifle-cartridge reloader. He helped me clamp the hardware to a worktable in my bedroom. "Dostoyevsky wasn't a pansy," he said.

Before I started reloading, I read a magazine on guns and ammunition. I memorized ballistics of rifle bullets: how fast they traveled out of the chamber, how many foot-pounds of energy they had on leaving the muzzle, how many inches they dropped after flying a thousand feet, how many miles they would cover before they hit the ground.

Armed with the information, I began to use the tool. I clamped the flange of an empty cartridge to the base of the reloader vise. I pulled the handle down, raising the cartridge to meet a rod. I forced the cartridge's neck over the rod, then brought the handle back.

I counted grains of gunpowder with a plastic spoon, then poured the powder into the stretched metal casing. I plugged a copper-jacketed slug into the open end, traded the extruder for a crimper, pulled the handle down, and locked the slug in.

I removed the cartridge from the vise and snapped in a firing cap.

I fetched a deer rifle that belonged to my father, opened the bolt, and slid the reloaded cartridge into the chamber. The shell was tight, but I was able to force the bolt closed. As long as the bolt was shut, I figured, I could fire the cartridge.

*

A girl from a neighboring high school invited me to her house to watch an eclipse of the moon. I asked my mother to give me a ride, and on the appointed evening she took me.

At the girl's house, I saw a chessboard on a low table and asked the girl's father if he wanted to play. After a few moves, he said, "You don't play this game much, do you?"

After dark, the girl and I looked out a narrow window, through the bare branches of a tree. A copper-colored shadow appeared at the bottom of the moon's disk, then moved slowly upward.

The girl brought out a lump of something that looked like dried rubber cement. The substance was soft, and its surface sparkled.

"What is it?" I asked.

"Opium," she said, "from a foreign den."

We smoked the wad in a tiny pipe. Though the fumes were fragrant and I puffed prodigiously, I failed to become any happier.

A while later, the moon had turned completely brown. Shortly, a sliver of light appeared at the bottom of the disk and expanded, pushing the shadow away.

The girl said, "I'm thinking of changing my name to Swamp. I'm going to travel south and major in math."

The moon was still behind the bare branches. "How often does this happen?" I asked.

"Here," she said, "once a century."

*

When I was ready to test-fire my reloaded cartridges, I went to look for my father. He was lying on his bed, with all of the shades pulled. An empty bottle stood on a clothes trunk next to him. Some sunlight was leaking in, so he kept one arm over his eyes.

"I have only twenty productive years left," he said. "And I haven't even started yet. It's because I have to spend my time taking care of kids."

*

I found my brother and sister and brought them with me to test the cartridges. We walked on a farm lane until we came to an abandoned iron-ore hole. People had dumped trash in the pit, and brush had grown up through the garbage.

I found some cans and bottles and set them on rocks. Then I stepped back and told my brother and sister to stand behind me.

I forced a wrinkled .30-caliber round into my father's rifle. I cocked the hammer and looked down the barrel. Then I thought of what could happen if the slug jammed in the chamber. If the exploding gas couldn't escape forward, it would blast backward, into my face.

I ejected the cartridge and put it in my pocket.

"Are you going to shoot?" my sister asked.

"No," I said.

"Then let's go," my brother said.

As we walked, I silently planned my next reloading session. I would use a smooth, quick vise motion, and I would pack the cartridges with extra grains. Back outside, I would not let my finger freeze on the trigger.

*

HOLIDAY SEASON

Before Christmas, my father took my brother and sister and me to a farm where we could cut down a tree. At the nursery, the hilly land was dotted with small pines growing in rows. The farm owner lent us a bow-shaped saw, and we carried it with us as we hiked over ground covered with a crust of ice.

When we came to a spruce specimen that seemed to have the right size and shape, I knelt on the ground and began to hack at the trunk. I worked my arm back and forth, and the saw teeth chewed through the sap-moistened wood. My brother helped with the job, while my sister hung back with my father. After the tree fell, we dragged it to the car and laced it onto the roof.

At home, the tree turned out to be bigger than it had seemed outside. Its top hit the living-room ceiling and curled, so the uppermost twig pointed down toward the floor.

We children plugged in a string of lights and admired the colored bulbs for a while as they lay in a pool; then we draped the electrical cord through the pine branches. We attached ornaments, including a starlike object that stuck out from the topmost branch at an odd angle.

When we had finished decorating, we switched on the television and watched a show. From where we were sitting, we could see the tree lights reflected in the picture tube.

My sister turned away from the television and said to me, "You know, I used to think that when I grew up, I would try to meet a boy who looked like you, but now I see that no one looks like you."

"Just wait," I said. "When that cowboy show comes on, the one with the father and three sons, you'll see that the ranch cook looks like me. His name is Hop Sing."

*

During the night, I heard the sound of breaking glass, and when I went to investigate, I saw that the Christmas tree had fallen over. My father was standing next to the tree; he looked like he'd just awakened. "The thing was leaning all night," he explained. "I was sitting here, drinking beer and watching it."

*

In the morning, my brother and sister and I picked up the lights, tinsel and ornaments, but we didn't put the decorations on the tree again. Instead, we dressed up a potted grapefruit tree that my mother had grown from a seed. The grapefruit tree was about three feet high, and it was scrawny, with snakelike branches and long spines. We wrapped a blanket around the flowerpot, looped lights between the waxy leaves, and hooked ornaments onto the twigs. In a way, the glass balls looked like citrus fruit.

*

For a Christmas present, my father gave me a patch cord for my flute. I screwed one end of the cord—the end with a microphone pickup—into the mouthpiece. Next, I looked for a receptacle for the jack. The problem was, I had no amplifier. So I plugged my electrified flute into my father's stereo system. When I blew across the mouthpiece with vibrato, I produced high-pitched feedback through the speakers.

I stood on one leg, with one foot resting on a knee, stork-like, and imagined that I was in a rock band. Then I ripped into a Bach sonata. All I needed was a guitarist, a bassist and a drummer to bring the music on home.

Unfortunately, the only accompanists I had were my brother on French horn and my sister on violin. "Let's play some Delta blues," I said.

We didn't know how to synchronize notes, but we tried to find a rhythm. We stuttered at first, and then we galloped along.

*

On New Year's Eve, my father called me into his workroom. He was sitting on a stool next to a metal-topped table. On the table, there were some dried butterflies pinned to fiberboard strips.

My father poured bourbon and cola into a glass and handed the drink to me. I sat on a chair, with my head below his.

He took an aluminum flask from a back pocket, gulped from the container, and started to talk. "When I was a kid," he said, "my sister and I spent a New Year's Eve together. We were by ourselves; the rest of the family was out. She told me she wanted to find a waveless bay, a place of calm. She was upset."

I drank the spiked cola.

"Not long after that," my father continued, "my sister killed herself. I was in the Army, and she wasn't much older than I was. She'd given me a wristwatch, and when I heard the news, I lost the timepiece. I spent hours retracing my steps, walking up and down a beach, but I never found the gift."

My father refilled my glass.

"Anyway," he said, "because of that, I changed my profession. I'd been a chemistry major; I'd been trying to invent a better toothpaste. But with my sister gone, I decided to become a revolutionary."

He slipped off his stool and, to steady himself, grabbed the nearest object, which happened to be a broomstick. "I'm armed," he said. "I'm a certified marksman. I got a medal in the service."

He waved the broom in the air. "I've got a Mauser," he shouted, "and three hollow-point rounds: one for the president, one for the vice president, and one for myself!"

*

I went to my bed and lay down. I felt as if I'd been twirling in place with my arms out. I could see the walls of my room revolving around me. I tried to stop the motion by moving my head in the opposite direction, but when my neck would twist no farther, the room began to spin again.

I tried to make myself throw up. I stuck a finger down my throat, but I couldn't poke deeply enough. As soon as I touched the hanging nodule at the back of my mouth, my throat clenched and ejected my fingertip. I choked and gagged but couldn't upchuck.

I went to sleep and woke soon after, feeling sick. I thought that the sensation would fade, that I could just go back to sleep. But as minutes passed, I felt more nauseated. I had to get out of bed and look for a place to throw up.

*

My mother told me I should make a resolution for the New Year. "When I was a child," she said, "we wrote our resolutions on paper. Then we burned the paper. It was like burning a model of the house of a person who'd just died. The spirit would rise with the smoke."

For my resolution, I wrote that I would try to prevent my father from assassinating the president and vice president. If I couldn't stop him, I would turn him in to the FBI.

I folded my statement, put it in an ashtray and touched a lit match to the paper.

*

VISITING ARTIST

When a friend of my father's came to visit, my father introduced him by saying, "We both went to each other's first art show. I was the only person at his show, and he was the only person at mine. Now, look where we are."

"Where are you?" my mother asked.

"I'm nowhere," my father said, "because I had to raise a family."

At dinner, the friend said, "I have only one testicle. The other got crushed when I crashed. I was racing my motorcycle, going around a turn. Suddenly, I was flying through the air.

"My nose was sewn back on and one of my eyebrows was reattached," he added. "I healed, but then I rode my motorcycle to the hospital for a checkup. On the way, I hit a puddle and broke my collarbone."

After dinner, the friend took me for a ride on his new bike. We didn't wear helmets, and he took curves at high speed. When I asked him how fast we were going around the turns, he said, "Eighty."

*

My father went out with the biker/artist, and when they came back, they were carrying a signboard with Greek letters on it.

"We went to a fraternity bar," my father said, "and they didn't like what I was saying. I was talking about that mountain man who kidnapped a teenager and shot three FBI agents and their dog when they came after him. That man was a hero."

"No one agreed," my father's friend said, "so we stole the fraternity sign."

*

In my unoccupied moments, I played with my navel. I poked a finger into it, looked into the crevices, used my nail. I wanted to explore the indentation. I kept at this until the inside area began to bleed.

After a time, the bleeding stopped, but I knew that I wouldn't let my navel heal. I would pick the scabs off, the skin would bleed again, and the scratches would crust over. Then I would poke at the dimple again.

*

While my father visited the local bar, his friend stayed in the house and played with a home-movie camera. He set the camera on a tripod and aimed the lens at the kitchen table. He took two plastic tusks from an unassembled dinosaur skeleton my father had given to me and clamped them between his teeth. The tusks stuck out of his beard and made him look fierce.

He picked up a teddy bear, laid it on a plate, and switched on the movie camera. He sat at the table with the bear in front of him and attacked the stuffed animal with a knife and fork.

He stopped the film, filled his plate with white dinosaur bones and rolled the camera again. He picked up the bones one at a time—a rib cage, a femur—and turned them back and forth in front of his face. Finding no meat, he threw the bones away.

*

My mother sent me to fetch my father at the bar. When I got there, my father told me to sit on a stool beside him. There were a few other men at the counter, but no one was talking. They were all watching a television that rested on a shelf near the ceiling.

"See those two guys," my father said to me. "Their names are Harry and Herbert Imp. They own a shack in a gap in the hills. I want to move there, away from you and your mother. You can have your moods—you can make demands and play with yourselves—but I won't be watching."

I looked across the room at the Imps, but they didn't acknowledge my presence.

*

When I was alone, I found a rubber band and wrapped it around my penis. I looped the band once around my entire basketry and snapped the leftover part onto the shaft. Save for the loss of a few pinched hairs, I was fine. I didn't think my banded root would die. In fact, whenever it started to wilt, it bounced right back.

I learned I could achieve the same effect with a piece of string, a hospital tourniquet, or a doubled hair Scrunchy. But I preferred to use a standard rubber band on my genitals.

Basically, I'd invented my own personal slingshot. I grabbed the handle, looped up the sling, snapped the elastic, and let the ever-tightening wrapper do its work.

*

My father told his friend that he should make a painting of my brother and sister and me. "You may as well catch them now," he said to his friend, "before they land in prison."

The three of us stood shoulder-to-shoulder in a doorway. We didn't move for about half an hour while the artist worked. When he was finished, he set his painting on the floor so it could dry.

When I looked at the image of myself and my siblings, I thought it was unflattering. My brother and I looked like apes, with our shoulders rounded and our arms hanging in front. My sister was wearing glasses that overwhelmed her face, and her lips were curled in a sneer.

When my father saw the painting, he said, "Those are my sullen children. When they don't get what they want, they sulk."

*

I found that if I stood on a chair, I could hang myself. I didn't want to hang myself by my neck, because that would have been too dangerous. So I hung myself by my wrists. I reached up, attached my hands to a rope above me, then stepped off the seat.

While I was afraid of getting caught, I was more afraid of getting stuck, of not being able to step back onto the chair. If, for example, I knocked the chair over when stepping off, I would be in trouble. I might not die for a long time, but I would be mighty uncomfortable.

*

At night, my mother came to the side of my bed and began to talk to me. I wanted her to leave, but I couldn't say so.

"I never wanted to kill myself," she said. "I always looked up at the sky, at the flying shapes and the Cloud Princess, and asked myself if I really wanted to die. Of course, if I did die, I might learn more about the clouds and the moon. But I decided to listen to the monks on the mountain instead. I could hear them chanting from anywhere in the city."

*

When my mother was gone, I took out a kaleidoscope, pointed it at the sky, and looked into the eyepiece. I twisted the light-catching end to mix the fragments of colored glass.

I centered the lens over the moon and saw the white disk shatter into diamonds and dots. With my free hand, I felt for my navel.

I didn't care about lunar phases or the Cloud Princess. I just wanted to see the splinters of white light up close, next to the sensor of my brain.

*

TETCHED

On a damp weekend day, my father took my siblings and me to the ridge behind town. The ground was spongy, and everything was lit gray. We were supposed to find wild asparagus, chop the stalks, and bring them home.

We walked up the first hill, searching in the tall grass for dark-green spears.

My father pointed out a feathery plant by the side of the trail—asparagus that had gone to seed. Near the base of the plant were a couple of shoots. We sliced them off and put them in a sack.

We walked back and forth along the ridge, bending weeds with our feet, but we found no more asparagus.

At home, my father combined our harvest with store-bought vegetables and said that he would make soup.

*

At dinner, my mother didn't eat with the rest of us. She stood to the side, with an apron on over her hospital uniform.

"Developers are ruining the farmland," my father said. "What we need is a peasant uprising. We need to overrun the aristocracy with tractors. That's why I'm going into politics, or at least into Washington."

After he'd finished speaking, he left by the side-porch door, heading presumably for the local bar, and my mother joined us at the table.

*

Another day, as I walked along the street by myself, I saw some children playing in a yard. They were running, chasing each other, but they stopped to look at me.

After I'd passed, I heard one of them call out, "Your father has syph!"

*

I saw my father lying on his bed with his arm over his eyes. His room was dark.

He started talking from behind his arm. "I'm in my prime," he said, "at the peak of my strength and productivity. But I don't spend my time making art, making revolution, setting up a new government. No, I spend it arguing with your mother and entertaining you.

"Tell me," he added, "do you have sex with your mother?"

I went downstairs and sat on the sofa with my brother and sister.

After a while, we heard our father coming down the steps. We looked at him and saw that he was carrying a roll of toilet paper. He followed our gaze and noticed the white tissue.

"I was reading a magazine in the bathroom," he said.

*

I walked outside and wandered until I heard the sounds of activity. A neighbor, I noticed, was having a party.

I stood, looking at people through the door, then went in.

A young man with long hair stared at me without speaking.

"Don't pay attention to him," someone said to me. "He's *tetched*."

All of the partyers were male. One of them, I understood, was getting married.

In a room without furniture, several men were sitting on the floor, playing cards. I sat with them and was dealt in, even though I didn't ante.

"To be a man," one of the players said, "you have to split a black oak."

"There are plenty of black oaks in the woods," another said.

"This oak isn't a tree," the first said, "but she is black and hard to split."

The second speaker reached over, grabbed the first one's crotch, tickled, and held on.

The first man scooted away. "I can tell that you sit to piss," he said.

"I have to sit to piss," the grabber said, "because my doctor told me I can't lift more than a hundred pounds."

When I was dealt a sure winner, I put down two dollars and lost.

*

"Let's go for a ride," the tetched young man said to me,

I got into the passenger seat of his pickup, and he took a bottle from under the driver's seat. I drank some sweet liquor and watched the scenery.

We stopped at a red light on a four-lane section of highway, and a car with a loud engine pulled up beside us.

"Sounds like a glass pack," my driver said.

He took hold of a handle under his dashboard. "See this?" he said to me. "It's a rip cord grip. I use it to attach the muffler to the engine."

When the light changed, we started drag-racing. I could feel our vehicle's acceleration, and I could see the pavement scrolling under us at an increasing rate. Each time a gear was changed, I sensed a pause and a thrust. The race lasted until we reached the next red light.

"Big deal," my driver said. "He beat a truck."

Turning to me, he said, "Pick up the CB microphone. Contact the airport and ask for clearance."

We covered several miles on twisting one-lanes, waiting for permission to touch down.

Presently, my pilot dropped me off at home.

*

A couple of days later, my mother came home from her hospital job and said to me, "I tested your father's blood."

"Why?" I asked.

"He had a boil that was making it hard for him to walk."

"How did you get his blood?" I asked.

"I stuck him."

"With a needle?"

"No, with a metal stick."

I didn't want to talk about the hospital test.

"He has syphilis," my mother said. "It's too late for incremental treatment. He needs a massive dose of drugs."

*

What I wanted to do was to hit myself, so I borrowed my sister's horse-riding crop. Then I removed some clothes and aimed for bare skin.

The problem was, I couldn't get a proper angle, or good leverage, to strike straight on. I couldn't swing the whip from my shoulder; I had to use my wrist.

I cracked at myself as hard as I could, and after a few minutes I saw double-sided welts, raised by the crop's steel armature.

Guessing I was kinky, knowing I was different, and resolving to keep my deviance very quiet, I kept going with the riding crop until I got bored.

*

I walked out to the highway after a storm. The air was damp and glowing with an orange light. I saw a car rolling toward me with its headlights on.

I saw a bolt of lighting jump from a low cloud to the roof of the car. Simultaneously, a spark flashed between the car's chassis and the pavement. The car's headlights went out, and the vehicle stopped suddenly.

I wondered if the driver was harmed, but I couldn't see in through the windows.

After a minute or so, the car started to move again. It gathered speed and rolled past me.

I waited for the next bolt to hit.

*

HUNTING FOR CLUES

I watched while my father restored a rusted gun. He split the trigger casing open to reveal the moving parts. With his fingers, he tested a small lever, rocking it on its pivot. "This gun belonged to my father," he explained. "It's a single-shot, so you have to make each trigger pull count."

Using a hand file, he sawed a notch into the metal part that held the trigger safety back. He worked for several minutes but hardly made a dent.

"The trigger will have a hair touch," he said, "but the gun probably won't go off while you're carrying it."

He slicked the steel with bluing oil and said, "You should read Che's diary. You have to make a commitment to fight. But you can forget about wearing a beret with a red star. That's for fashionistas, not Zapatistas."

"I have an arsenal in my art studio," he continued. "I won't be taken alive."

He handed me the gun. "When the revolution comes, you'll need it," he said. "In the meantime, use it for rabbits."

*

I picked up the single-shot blunderbuss, put on my hunting coat and boots, and walked to the overgrown hill behind town. As I trudged, I thought about the gun's safety. I pictured my father's filed notch holding back the firing pin.

I kicked at grass and weed patches and plowed through briars, letting the thorns slide into my denim pants. When I grew tired of flailing, I stopped to rest. At that moment, I heard a drumming and saw a ring-necked pheasant flush up. Against the expanse of field and weeds, the bird looked huge. I raised my gun, swung the barrel in an arc, led the bird with the bead, and fired my one shot.

The blast wiped out my senses, and for an instant all I could see was smoke. Then I saw the pheasant, wings outstretched, gliding downward. I rushed to reload: I broke the gun, slid in a shell, shut the action. Meanwhile, the pheasant disappeared into the tall straw-colored grass.

On my way back home, I put my weight on a heel over a patch of mud while walking downhill. My feet slid out from under me, and I pitched forward. My gun hit the ground before my hands, and the loaded 16-gauge cartridge exploded. Fortunately, the muzzle was pointed away.

*

I got a ride with a teenaged boy who was driving a pickup truck. He followed double tire tracks along the perimeters of fields as he headed toward town. Steering with one hand, he took a bottle from under the car seat. "Do you want some Mad Dog?" he asked.

I accepted the bottle, then gave it back to him.

As we passed a farmhouse, he asked, "Do you know the redheaded twins who live there?"

I knew the twins' names, and I knew what they looked like. "Yes," I said.

"They're nice," he said. "But they never come out of their house. Girls are scarce around here. That's why I have sex with guys."

"How do you do that?" I asked.

"Two ways. Face-to-face and face-to-back, both times rubbing."

"Which guys?" I asked.

"Strong ones. Guys who can do one-handed pull-ups and strangle cows."

"Where?" I asked.

"Mostly in the back of the truck."

I felt the Mad Dog turning things in reverse in my mind. "What if your penis isn't the right shape?" I asked.

"Mine curves up, and the tip looks like a mushroom cap. But one of the guys I know has a boner tapered like a spear."

At home, I examined my rubbing instrument. It resembled neither a mushroom nor a spear. In fact, it curved downward, though it could be bent upward. Either way, its length was not as impressive as it would have been if the shaft were plumb.

Obviously, my bow-shaped prong had been restricted too long. I threw away all of my briefs-style underwear.

*

Late in the evening, my mother came home from visiting a man she worked with at the hospital. My father had been drinking while she was out.

"Where were you?" my father asked her.

"At Mr. Supansky's."

"What were you doing at Mr. Asspansky's?" my father asked.

"Talking about my blood-count equation," my mother said. "I developed it for my work in the lab. I call it my madness."

"Did Mr. Asspansky think you were crazy?" my father asked.

"No, he sold me a flute for our son."

"You were playing the skin flute!" my father shouted. "And you want to teach our son to play the skin flute?"

"No, I wasn't," my mother said. "And his name is Mr. Supansky."

"Was his skin flute long and strong?" my father asked.

*

I took a look at the flute my mother had gotten. It had closed keys and was made of silver, with a nickel mouthpiece. I didn't put the three parts of the flute together. Instead, I picked up the mouthpiece section and blew across the airhole. The tone was rich and mellow, like the sound from an empty bottle. I flapped my palm against the open end to create a tremolo.

"We didn't have flutes where I grew up," my mother said to me. "We had the *pi-pa*. The player practiced in the forest. The sound of the *pi-pa* string was the perfect music for pandas munching bamboo leaves. Of course, the plucking drowned out the chewing."

*

On a class trip to the library, I found a book on local history. I turned to a chapter on atrocities committed by native Americans. The Nitta-nees had done horrible things to early settlers. The worst practice, to my mind, was burying people up to their necks and building a fire around their heads. A group of settlers had met this fate, except for one woman. She had escaped burial and burning—but had not escaped being stripped naked. She ran nude from the natives' enclave and hid in the woods. After twenty days of wandering, she was found, undraped but alive, in the hollow trunk of a tree.

I checked the book out of the library and brought it home. Then I went to visit the redheaded twins.

"What are you doing here?" one of them asked.

"Do you know about the local Indians?" I asked.

"We can't come out, and you can't come in," she said.

"I'll just sit here," I said.

I waited outside, reading about white slavery in the tribal world, until the twins' mother came out.

"I want to make a film," I told her, "called *Indian Captive*."

"You're the rudest boy I've ever met," she said.

Shortly afterward, my father came to get me.

"I think I'll go away to college," I said to him.

"You shouldn't do that," he said. "You should buy a secondhand van and drive around the country. You can do some drinking and thinking, and nobody will bother you. You won't be able to bathe often, but nobody will care. You might even have time to write down your thoughts while you recover from your hangovers."

*

"You have to forgive your father," my mother said to me. "He was unhappy as a child because his own father was successful.

"He went to college on the G.I. Bill," my mother continued, "but all he wanted to do was set off bombs in the chemistry lab. He would mix up saltpeter, put it on a piece of paper, and tap it—*tap, tap, tap*. The powder would explode while the teacher was lecturing.

"He quit chemistry to avoid making toothpaste. He switched to painting to stay out of the lab."

*

I walked to the lowland near the town's creek to scout locations for *Indian Captive*. I found an elevated spot for a sacred house, an Appalachian kiva. The house would be entered by climbing a ladder, then stepping through a hole in the roof. Nearby, I found two parallel trees about six feet apart, perfect for holding the captive while I conducted the inquisition. There would be no need for burning or killing, but the interrogation would go on for hours.

As I walked, I kicked through large leaves of plants I thought were rhubarb. I was glad to have made the discovery, because rhubarb was edible. But when I looked closely, I saw that the stems of the plants were green, not red, and realized I was in a patch of skunk cabbage. When I crushed the plants, they gave off an unpleasant organic smell.

*

At home, I picked up my new flute, opened sheet music to an étude, sat on the edge of my bed, and played. My fingering was fairly exact, but my tone was whistly. After a while, I heard what I thought were birds answering me.

*

INTO THE COLD

When I got home from school, my first job was to stoke the furnace. Because I was older than my sister and brother, I supposedly was best able to handle the task.

My parents hadn't arrived yet, and the house was cold, so I kept my coat on and went to the woodshed. I opened the door to the furnace room—a large closet divided from the shed—and switched on the light. The furnace seemed dead: I heard no snapping and felt no heat. I opened the middle door of the large cast-iron stove and looked inside. There was a heap of coal ash, no unburned chunks. I reached to the side, grabbed the long, metal lever, and worked it back and forth. The ashes quaked and settled as I opened and closed the louvered grate. After a while, some glowing coals appeared.

I picked up a shovel and went into the main part of the woodshed. In a boarded stall, coal was piled below a loading hole. I scooped up some lumps and threw them into the furnace. I was careful not to put on too many, because they could suffocate the fire.

*

Inside, my brother and sister were watching a gothic soap opera on television. They were wearing their coats.

"Did you feed the furnace?" they asked.

"Yes," I said.

I put my hand around a copper pipe that carried steam to the upstairs rooms. The pipe felt cold, but I kept my hand around it until it began to get warm.

"I don't want our father to come home," my sister said.

"Why not?" I asked.

"The other day, when no one else was home, I heard him taking a bath. I went upstairs; I was just going to my room. But when I got to the hallway, he opened the bathroom door and said,

'Come in.' I looked in and saw him in the tub. 'Let's play a game,' he said."

"Did anything happen?" I asked.

"Not that time, but lots of things have happened. I don't know why he's always demanding to know that I'm not pregnant. I could get pregnant."

*

When my father got home, he said, "I'm tired of the rat race. I'm tired of working for capitalists. I want to invent the next Hula-Hoop."

Shortly afterward, my mother arrived from work. When she walked in, my father asked her if he could borrow some money. She gave him a couple of bills, and he left the house. I guessed he was heading for the local bar.

*

I caught a ride with my mother when she took the family's laundry to town. On the way, she said, "Soon, it will be Chinese New Year, but this isn't your year. You'll have to wait eight more years. Then the Horse will gallop in."

I didn't stay at the wash shop with my mother. Instead, I walked to the movie theater.

There were a couple of students from my high school in the audience. I sat at the border of the group, next to a girl.

"Where were you born?" she asked.

"Here," I said. "I was born here."

"Oh," she said, "I thought you were Japanese."

"My mother came here for college," I said.

The movie was a ghost story, set on an estate. The lady of the estate suffered from paranoia and unexpected visions. At one point, she woke and saw her gardener climbing in through her window. He pulled her from her bed and hogtied her on the carpet. But he didn't molest her; he just took advantage of her arched position by rocking her on her stomach and speaking softly while she sobbed. He left quickly, but didn't untie her before he left.

I put my hand on the knee of the girl next to me. She was wearing jeans, but I could feel warmth through the denim. I took her hand, and she squeezed back with her fingers.

Later, I asked if she wanted to go out another time, and she said, "I wouldn't mind, but I don't know what my parents would think. We're Methodists, you know."

*

When I got home, I saw my father drinking in the kitchen. He was using a pint mug and a shot glass. On the table were a couple of empty beer bottles, a couple of full ones, and a half-full bottle of bourbon. He was sitting sideways in his chair; he seemed about to fall from the seat.

When he saw me, he straightened up. "I can't wait for you kids to move out," he said. "Then I can stop being a wage slave. I can get back to my real work. I wasn't meant to support a family. I was meant to create art."

"Where would I go?" I asked.

"I don't care," he said. "Buy yourself a van and sleep in the back. You can go anywhere you damn well please. ...."

"What about college?" I asked.

"Don't go to college. Go to vocational school. Study auto mechanics. That way, you can fix your van when it breaks down."

"I don't think I can afford a vehicle," I mumbled.

"Then use your thumb!"

*

In my bedroom, I lit a stick of incense and took out a plastic pouch of tobacco. I rolled a pinch of shredded leaves into a cigarette, then lit it. The fumes made my head swim. I thought I could smoke one stick and stop, maybe for days, but as soon as I had finished the cigarette, I rolled another and smoked it.

I read some letters I'd received from colleges. The solicitations came from scientific-sounding schools: an institute of technology, a polytechnic university. These subjects, like auto mechanics, didn't interest me. I thought I had something personal to say. I decided to concentrate less on numbers and focus more closely on self-expression.

My mother looked in through my doorway. "Here's my advice," she said. "Follow the sounds of the reed flute through the bamboo trees. When you reach the source, you'll know the song."

*

In the morning, I saw frost on the inside of my windows and hurried to get dressed. I looked out at the empty street and, with a fingernail, scratched some trails through the ice on the glass. I looked in the mirror and saw my mother's Asian features on my face.

*

At school, I saw the girl I'd sat with at the movie.

"I want you to do me a favor," she said. "I want you to take a note from me and give it to a boy I like."

She held out a folded sheet of paper.

"I don't want to do that," I said.

"I'll beg you," she said.

She dropped to her knees. She was wearing high socks and loafers, and the hem of her skirt didn't reach the floor. When she bent her toes to keep her balance, I could see pennies in the slots of her shoes. She walked on her knees to get closer to me. She put her hands together, locked her fingers, and looked up at me.

"Please," she said.

I took the note from her.

*

When I got home from school, I found the furnace fire totally out, so I tried to restart it with crumpled newspaper and kindling. The wood caught, but the pieces of coal I put on would not burn. They smoldered without flame. The kindling fire was not hot enough to heat the house.

Inside, my brother and sister were wearing coats and sitting next to an electric heater. A new installment of the same gothic soap opera was on television. I joined them at the heater and leaned in toward the glowing elements. I was careful not to get too close, because I didn't want to burn my hair off.

*

In my room, I removed my clothes, except for my boxers. I took a piece of rope from a hiding place, tied my ankles together, and hopped into bed. I pulled up the covers and lay there. I planned to stay that way all night. I thought I deserved it.

Suddenly, my brother came into my room. The door hadn't been shut, because my father didn't allow closed doors.

My brother was excited. He didn't say anything; he just ripped the bedding off me. When he saw that my feet were tied together, he looked at my face and said, "Oooh."

*

LESSON PLAN

I picked out a couple of colleges that were located hundreds of miles from home and applied for admission.

Not long afterward, one of the places asked me to come for an interview. I made the trip by bus and met with a woman in a student lounge. She sat on a couch, and I sat on a chair, facing her.

As I talked, she began to doze off. She closed her eyes and leaned over until she was reclining on the couch cushions. Her breathing became slow and regular.

When I stopped talking, she woke and sat up. "Is there a lot of apathy in your high school?" she asked.

I started to answer, but as I spoke, she lost consciousness again. I didn't wake her. I just stood up and tiptoed out of the room.

*

At home, my father handed me a magazine photo of Che Guevara. The photo didn't actually show Guevara; it showed his corpse. The picture had been taken after he'd been killed by U.S. and Bolivian soldiers. He was naked from the waist up, and his eyes were open. His long hair and extended arms made him look like a jungle Messiah.

"Che died for your sins," my father said.

*

My father took me to a political demonstration. The night before, we joined our protest group in a nearby student union. Rock bands with names like Barefoot in Athens and Corduroy Road played while young dissidents sat on the floor or slept in quilted bags. In the early morning, all of us got on buses and headed for the capital.

Our group marshal was a meteorology student with an Afro haircut and a black armband. He told us we belonged to the New Mobilization, or New Mobe, unit.

In Washington, we walked along a tree-lined street filled with demonstrators. Our marshal led us in a call-and-response chant:
  "What do we want?" he shouted.
  "Peace!"
  "When do we want it?"
  "Now!"
  "What?"
  "Peace!"
  "When?"
  "Now!"
  "Peace now!"
  "Peace now!"
  As we walked across the central mall, I looked up and saw a young woman sitting in the crook of a tree. She was wearing blue jeans and holding a cardboard sign with the name of a college on it.
  Around me, I saw couples holding hands. I stared at one couple sharing a piece of chewing gum. One of them would chew for a while, then would remove the wad and give it to the other. After a time, the new chewer would eject the gum and return it.
  Downtown, I saw soldiers standing on rooftops. They were carrying long guns and grenade tripods. Occasionally, one of them would launch a gas canister, but none of the projectiles came my way.
  In the evening, I walked with my father back to the New Mobe bus. The air was chilly, and someone started a scrap-wood fire on the ground next to the vehicle. We stood near the flames and warmed our hands until it was time to board.

                              *

  Later, my father criticized our protest group. "The New Mobe," he said loudly, "is old news. That bus marshal was no meteorologist. He can't forecast the end of the war. He's full of hot air.
  "Che was a real revolutionary," my father added. "He didn't want to work for a newscast. He wanted to wipe out his enemies."

                              *

I went to a meeting so I could learn how some young men had managed to avoid getting drafted.

One speaker said that he'd gone underweight. He was six feet tall, and he weighed 110 at his physical exam. That was too light to pass.

Another resister said, "You can swallow a bottle of aspirin and drink lots of cola before your blood test. You'll register positive for leukemia."

"You can chop off a toe," another man said. "You can't fight a war with nine toes."

"Or you can claim you're a conscientious objector," said another. "Just don't wait till after you've enlisted to do it."

"You can write a letter of refusal to your draft board," someone else said. "You'll get three years for declining to register. You'll get your head bashed. But when you get out of jail, you can go back to school."

*

Another college invited me for an interview.

On the campus, a student asked me, "Do you have parents?"

"Yes," I said, "but they're not here."

I was wearing a plaid-wool jacket with a hunting license pinned to the back. The getup embarrassed me.

During the tour, the student focused on the school's Asian studies program. "We offer a workshop in feng shui," he said. "In that class, you sit facing the window. You see nature, but you can still hear the teacher."

After the tour, I followed a path through trees and found a small bridge over a gorge. As I stood there, a young woman came toward me and stopped. "Are you a graduate student?" she asked.

"No," I said.

As we talked, we looked through wire mesh at a creek below. At one point, we pressed our fingers into each other's palms. Before we parted, she gave me her address.

*

I made elaborate plans to visit her. I wanted to take a bus, spend one night, and return home the next day.

When I told my mother what I wanted to do, she said,
"There's plenty of time for floating down the river. Don't decorate
your canoe until you're older."

*

When I told my father I wanted to enter college, he said, "It
won't do you much good. Look at what it did for me. I'm a
chauffeur for my children."

Later, he asked, "What are you going to study?"

"Fine arts," I said.

"Really?" he said. "I think Che minored in art. You might be
able to spend a semester in Cuba. I'll help you get to Havana."

*

At night, I woke and looked out my bedroom window. I
could see the clearing next to the elementary school. Red lights
glowed there, and I spotted a running Ferris wheel. A carnival was
being held in the schoolyard.

I rose from bed and got dressed. The time was 3 or 4 a.m.

When I walked out of my room, my mother noticed that I
was leaving. "Where are you going?" she asked.

"To the carnival," I said.

"Don't cross the fence," she said, "until you count three
moons."

I went back to my room and looked out the window, but the
opening was below me now, at the bottom. I could see the walls
around me, and I could hear the sound of machinery.

I tried to shout, "Ma!" but the word was drowned out. I tried
to set the window straight out in front of me, but I couldn't
because I was almost falling through it.

I scanned the sky and counted just one moon.

*

LAUGH TRACK

I heard music coming from a nearby dorm room, so I opened my door and looked out. In the hallway, students had tied plastic bags to the sprinklers, then lit the bags. They were watching flaming drops of plastic fall into a bucket of water. The drops made whizzing sounds as they shot through the air.

The music was coming from a neighbor's room. I walked to the source of the noise, looked in and saw a few young people smoking marijuana.

I wanted to say, "Please be quiet. I need to get some sleep for an exam" or "If you don't shut up, I'll call the cops," but instead I said, "Those leaves smell like they were grown on foreign soil."

One of the students looked at me and said, "I know you. When I saw your name in the freshman directory, I thought you'd look like a football player. Then I saw your photo."

"My father sent it," I said.

"Your photo is, bar none, the worst in the book."

My colleagues were playing Russian roulette with a marijuana cigarette. They were using two unlit matches for a holder as they passed the butt end around. They were waiting to see when the matches would ignite in someone's face.

After a few turns, the matches flared up under the nose of a student called Haystack. His hair, I noticed, fell in sheaves around his head. Some stray strands sizzled from the match fire, and he swatted them out. He didn't get upset; he just said, "I'm glad I didn't burn my hair off."

I sat on a mattress covered with an Army-green blanket. A young woman was sitting on the far end of the bed. "I found a poem taped to my door," she said. "It was in German, but I'm a German major, so I could read it. It went: 'Death is a master from Deutschland/He shouts, 'Play death more sweetly.' '"

"Who wrote it?" I asked.

"Paul Celan."

"I mean the note."

"I don't know."

"What does it mean?"

"Someone is trying to kill me! Death is playing more sweetly!"

"Who could that be?" I asked.

"I have some ideas," she said. "I saw a maniac in the library. He asked to borrow a pen from me. Later, I saw a light in the biology lab. I'm sure it was the same guy, working on a twisted experiment—sticking my pen into a doll that looked like me!"

At that point, I had a giggling fit. Nothing really provoked me, except for the image I had of myself inhaling deeply, then holding my breath while smoke leaked from my nostrils and tears dripped down my cheeks.

I exhaled through grinning teeth, then wailed like a banshee. I also looked like a banshee, because I had long hair that was held in place by a magical deerskin headband. Or at least this was how I envisioned a banshee. In any event, regardless of my headgear, I fell off my seat and onto the floor. I folded up like a fetus, rolled, twitched and kicked.

My jag was totally incapacitating. The more I tried to control it, the more unmanageable it became.

I had to leave the room so that those present would not witness my *petit mal* seizure. Alone, I giggled harder, thinking about the people waiting for me—people who most likely were not laughing at all, who most probably were hiding the weed, then getting ready to lie to me when I got back.

"There's none left," they said when I returned.

"You've got to be funnin' me," I said.

"No," they said. "You smoked the entire stash, like a fiend."

This downer of an announcement did not put me out of my comedy. I doubled over, tried to speak. I gestured weakly, quaked, fell to my hands and knees.

"You think I'm *non compos mentis*," I gasped.

" 'Fraid so," my friends said.

"There's nothing wrong with me," I said between hacks. "I'm perfectly normal."

I made a supreme effort to present a mature demeanor. But I was able to sit still for only a second or two before my composure crumbled.

When the gales hit again, nothing could douse my laughter burner. I gassed up on giggle fuel and followed a zigzag path to ultimate mirth.

*

The campus police came to my dorm floor. They said they were investigating a death threat.

"Is anyone here studying German-language poetry?" they asked.

They noticed a large carbon splotch on the hallway ceiling and asked what had happened, but no one would admit to attaching plastic bags to the sprinkler pipe and burning them.

Next, the cops looked into my neighbor's room and saw marijuana plants. They also spotted stolen lab glassware that had been fashioned into a water pipe.

The police took the plants and the bong. After they left, my neighbor tore apart his furniture. He scraped together some marijuana seeds and smoked them. "They're harsh," he said, "but they work."

*

Later, a young woman who lived upstairs confessed to taping the German poem to the other young woman's door. She insisted that she'd meant it as a gesture of good will, because she was a German major, too, and knew what it was like to be nutsoid the best part of the time.

*

FOOD FOR THOUGHT

To stretch our food money, my college roommate and I made gallons of orange juice from quart containers of concentrate. When we had guests, we would serve them the mixture. "There's plenty," we would say as we held out a gallon jug filled with pale-orange liquid.

Our guests would say, "This is good, but it tastes weak."

"If you drink more," we would say, "it's really tangy!"

*

My roommate and I prepared only two dishes, which we shared with each other on alternate days. One was pasta with tomato sauce, thickened with onion. The other was canned chow mein served over rice.

Between dinners, we ate peanut butter-and-jelly sandwiches.

My roommate claimed he'd eaten only eggs before he moved in with me. He'd boiled or fried them, then washed them down with water. He'd gone through a dozen eggs a day.

We used food stamps to pay for provisions. When our coupon allotment came through, the first items we bought were ten-pound bags of rice and onions. Then we loaded up on pasta, tomato sauce, chow mein and PB&J.

*

We made sculptures from the trash we generated. We were art majors, after all. For one piece, my roommate coated the inside of a grated-cheese jar with green ink. The intense color, seen through the glass, made the red letters of the brand name stand out.

Another time, I wrapped some uneaten spaghetti in plastic and froze it. The hardened dish retained its bright-orange color, and the shiny wrapping made it look crystalline, like a geological specimen.

*

One night, a couple of friends came to our place to play cards. My roommate and I made a special dish: chopped meat mixed with powdered extender, served over macaroni.

Before our game of Hearts, my roommate rolled a marijuana cigarette. The doobie was as thick as a cigar.

We played for a while, until one of the friends, without warning, threw up on the table. I couldn't understand why he didn't just get up and walk to the toilet, or at least to the kitchen sink, which was right behind him.

"It was the leaf," he explained. "I swallowed something green. I can't eat anything green. I had to bring it up."

"Why couldn't you have eaten the Queen of Hearts instead?" someone asked.

Later, the sick person lay down on a mattress and fell asleep. Someone found a can of shaving cream and covered him with white foam.

When the sleeper finally woke, he didn't get angry. He just brushed the foam off his clothing, put on his coat, and left.

*

On another occasion, I invited a female student for dinner. After the spaghetti and orange juice, she said, "You know, you could go to the supermarket and buy something like tuna fish. That would be a change for the better. Besides, it contains fish protein, which is healthier than meat protein."

"I'd rather survive on cigarettes and coffee," I said.

"You're a scary person," she said.

*

My roommate and I staged an art show in a student community center. We filled a wood-paneled room with painted food containers and frozen leftovers. For hors d'oeuvres, we served PB&J.

One of our art teachers came to the opening, surprising everyone with her presence. After viewing the inked grated-cheese jar and the hardened spaghetti, she said, "Anyone can do this kind of thing, but the refreshments aren't bad."

At that point, I seriously thought about changing my major, or at least adding some classes that suited me better.

*

Before the semester's last class, I smoked a marijuana bone outside a university hall. Then I went into a writing workshop, took a seat, and tried to look sober.

I saw that the teacher had brought a cake to celebrate. Students were taking turns slicing off pieces.

When the cake came to me, I lost the slicing knife; then I lost the platter. I found a sheet of cardboard and put the cake on that. I picked up a ruler and used it as a cutter. I slid the cake across the table to another student. Then I handed over the ruler.

I ate my cake off a piece of typing paper.

*

Later, I moved into a macrobiotic house, where no meat was allowed.

My new roommates and I belonged to a food co-op. On weekends, we would go to a retail distribution site—somebody else's house—where we sorted individual orders into grocery bags. Or we would go to the main distribution center—an airplane hangar—and divide up truckloads of produce. In return, we could buy our own groceries at low prices.

We made dishes out of vegetables and cheeses, and served them over bulgur, millet and other grains. For a while, I didn't know the word for millet. I called it "tiny yellow spheres" until a roommate corrected me.

Sometimes, we made yogurt by putting milk in the oven. We let the liquid curdle, then added a spoonful of commercial yogurt to introduce the right bacteria. We argued over whether the rotting milk smelled good or bad.

Once, one of my housemates caught me storing a package of chopped meat in the refrigerator. In response, she started to bang a frying pan against a kitchen counter. She whaled away until she put a dent in the utensil.

The strict food plan matched my roommates' radical sexuality. All intimacy was supposed to be politically correct. Patriarchy and persecution belonged on the compost heap.

As often as possible, I would sneak out for sausage heroes and pizza at the local grill. After I'd chowed down, I would go back home and eat healthy for as long as I could before I escaped for my next grease fix. My favorite sandwich was a meat-and-mushroom combo called a Suicide.

*

ACIDOPHILIA

A college friend asked me to travel overseas with him. "We can stay with my family," he said. "They won't hinder us."

Before we left, I watched while he sewed some doses of LSD into a shoe. He cut open the sole with a knife and inserted a blotter strip stained with blue dots. Then he sewed the leather shut.

When we arrived at the airport gate, a security guard took my friend aside.

When my friend returned, he said to me, "They made me take everything out of my pockets. They examined all of my belongings. They looked everywhere, except for my shoes!"

*

At his family's home, my friend unstitched his shoe sole and put the blotter strip in his parents' freezer. "If you don't freeze it," he explained, "the acid will degrade into strychnine. It will poison you like a rat."

*

In the evening, my friend's father invited us to take a sauna with him. The three of us went down to the basement and stripped off our clothes. Then we stepped into a wooden box.

Inside, there was a lightbulb, a wraparound bench and a small furnace. I sat on one side, facing the naked father and son.

"Is it hot enough?" the father asked.

"I don't think it is," my friend said. "The oven is fucked up."

"Can you use another word?" his father asked.

"The oven is screwed up."

His father threw a cup of water onto the furnace, and steam filled the tiny space. Sweat beaded on my skin, my eyes started to water, and my testicles shrank to the size of peanuts.

"When you can't stand it anymore," the father said, "just get out and go to the shower. Turn on the cold water, only the cold. Get soaked and come back."

I bolted from the box and raced for the shower. I could have cheated and turned on the warm water, but I didn't. I let the icy blast hit me. I started to shake, and my testicles shrank to the size of raisins.

I ran back to the box.

We repeated the sauna routine until all of our testicles disappeared.

*

I woke in the night and saw that my friend's bed was empty.

I saw light coming from downstairs, so I walked down the steps and looked into the kitchen.

My friend was sitting on the floor with a screwdriver in his hand. The refrigerator door was open, and the ice compartment lay in pieces on the floor. My friend looked at me with alarm and said, "I thought you were my father!"

"Don't worry," I said.

"The blotter fell into a crack," he said, "I had to take everything apart to find it."

*

The next day, he and I cut the rescued blotter strip into squares with scissors and swallowed a couple of the wafers with water. After a while, we both felt fine. We felt so fine we didn't think the drug was working. So we swallowed some more.

*

A young woman named Renatli came to visit, and the three of us went into my friend's bedroom.

"*Sprechen Sie Deutsch?*" she asked me.

"Only English," I said.

"*Nur Englisch?*" she said. "*Hasta la vista, turista!*"

When Renatli lit a cigarette, I couldn't take my eyes off it. I found a sheet of typing paper and started to draw with a ballpoint pen. I drew Renatli's hand, her fingers tweezing the burning stick. I drew the rising smoke, making curlicues for the wisps. I outlined her hair, face and body.

When she saw the drawing, she said, "I look like an eraser."

When I looked again, I saw that she indeed looked like a piece of rubber.

Soon, she said she had to leave.

"No!" my friend and I said. "You can't leave!"

"Why not?" she asked.

"We can't be alone!"

She stayed, and all of us sat and looked at each other without speaking for a couple of hours.

*

After she'd left, my friend and I were still awake, tripping.

"Will this ever end?" I asked.

"Not for a long time," my friend said.

"Maybe it's already over," I said. "Maybe everything will be like this for the rest of our lives."

"Like what?" he asked.

"Everything's unreal, but we can't remember what's real, so whatever's unreal will be real."

"That would be unbearable," he said.

*

I went to my bed and lay down, but I couldn't sleep. When I heard people moving around the house, I was sure they were crawling on their hands and knees, like animals.

*

In the morning, my friend and I joined his family for breakfast. We sat at a large table with his mother and sisters. We didn't mention that we'd been awake all night, and no one seemed to notice that we hadn't slept.

I wasn't hungry, so I just sat quietly.

"We're going for a walk," my friend said.

He and I went out a back door and up a hill covered with snow. At the top of the hill, we turned and looked back at the house. There was a large window across the wall of the kitchen, but we couldn't see into it. We stood in the snow, shivering.

When we got back, my friend's mother and sisters were waiting for us. "Did you have a nice walk?" they asked.

"Yes," we said.

"We saw you through the window," they said. "You looked a little lost, standing out there."

*

I wanted to see Renatli, so I called her and asked for directions. To get to the meeting place, I had to take stairs from the top of a mountain to its foot. Then I had to cross a square, pass a fountain, and climb up the side of another mountain.

At the designated spot, Renatli lit a cigarette and offered me one. Even though I had quit smoking, I joined her. My cigarette was excellent. I knew I wouldn't quit again for a very long time.

*

The next time my friend dropped acid, he did it with Renatli, not with me. While they were hallucinating together, I contemplated going home.

*

In the airport on my way back, a man in a trench coat asked me to follow him. He took me to a small room without windows. Inside, he asked, "What are you carrying in your pockets?"

I took out a couple of sugar cubes wrapped in paper. The man unpeeled a wrapper and looked at a white nugget. "Do kids still take acid these days?" he asked.

"Of course not," I said.

"You may as well tell me where the drugs are," the man said. "Don't make me find them."

I stood silently while the man looked into another pocket and found a twig. It was a stem with dry flowers—a souvenir. He looked at the plant, then opened a door to admit a dog. He held the twig under the dog's nose, and the dog sniffed vigorously at the wilted object.

The agent kept the twig and sugar, then released me to my own country.

*

DREADED SPERM BUILDUP

Most days, I struggled with the buildup of sperm. I couldn't ignore the fact that, out of neglect, my testes ached most of the time. It wasn't that I didn't want to release the trapped flagellates; I just didn't want to be caught doing the releasing.

Sometimes, my forgotten penis would rise during a lecture. Since my pants were tight, there was nowhere for the extension to go. My tool stayed restricted while I listened to the professor, who always seemed to dwell on obscure details, related in the loosest way to the primary source. I couldn't concentrate on textual compression theory when all I could think about was sperm bursting to be free.

*

My main romantic activity was listening to my apartment mate have sex with his girlfriend. When they copulated, I couldn't shut them out. He was silent, but her voice rose in volume as her notes traveled up the scale. I would sit and smoke a cigarette while I listened.

Once, in the middle of a sex recital, the phone rang in the hallway and my apartment mate stepped out to answer it. When he saw me, he put his finger to his lips and said, "Shhh."

I waited for his girlfriend to follow him out of the room, but she never showed.

*

Driven by my horrible hormonal imperative, I went on a date with a classmate. After we saw a movie, we went to her room. There, we ended up on the floor next to her bed.

Unfortunately, I didn't know what to do. I didn't know whether to stick my toe in her ear, or my finger in her nose, or keep my hands and feet to myself. So I fell back on lip action.

She seemed interested in this activity, but I should have known that she really wasn't. I had never experienced disinterested compliance before, so I interpreted her detachment as encouragement. I was so taken by the novelty that I was unaware of my own neutrality.

*

Days later, she came to my room after midnight. She hadn't said she would visit, so I was surprised to see her.

"Can I stay with you tonight?" she asked.

"Of course," I said.

I went to bed, and she arrived at the side of my mattress in a nightgown. The garment was slippery, and the hem reached to her knees. She lay next to me, then turned away. I tried to pull her closer, but I couldn't budge her. I knew then that I was sharing my bed with a dead fish, a large, smooth specimen. But I didn't know why the fish had expired.

I didn't realize that my companion was visiting not because she wanted to see me, but because the person she really wanted to see didn't want to see her. By the time she explained, I was too frustrated to care.

*

The sperm buildup had begun.

I dreaded the upsurge, because it invariably led me to a zone between composure and insanity.

*

I raided the public laundry. I left my apartment and went directly to the basement. By the time I entered the room with the washer and dryer, I was trembling. When I saw a load in the tumbler, I knew I'd struck gold.

I made sure no one was looking, then I opened the door to the dryer and took out a pair of socks. They were warm, somewhat damp, and, most important, soft and fuzzy. The fact that these socks belonged to a stranger gave me the shakes.

Socks in pocket, I raced up to my apartment, ripped open the door and slipped inside. I took out my booty, had a sniff, then a rub, then said to myself, "Sock it to me!"

I wasted no time in defiling the socks. I nibbled them with my lips, soaked them with my spit, then took out my argyle buster and worked them over till they needed patches.

When I was totally spent, I returned them to the dryer. The machine was still running, so I threw them in.

Then I made a vow never to steal socks again. But I knew it wouldn't be long before I was back to sock stalking. My sock drawer was bursting with loot.

*

The next time I ran into my classmate, she asked, "Where have you been?"

I didn't want to tell her that I had been avoiding her deliberately, that anytime I had an urge to contact her, I stopped myself from calling.

"I've been home," I said, "doing homework."

"Oh," she said. "I thought you'd dropped out of school."

I said something about textual compression theory, but didn't say anything about the socks.

*

TICKLED PINK

I didn't get much bondage in college. No, I spent most of my time studying, sitting in carrels, and searching the card catalogs for monographs on the topic of restraint. But I rarely found any articles on strings and straps as sex enhancers. An article on knots turned out to be a guide to Boy Scout techniques; a treatise on rigging focused on mainsails and jibs. I hungered for any iota of bondage data.

Outside the library, I attempted to sustain my fixation. At my lonely, off-campus desk, I skimmed the classics for kinky passages. The closest I found was a stanza in a Homeric epic. While armies fight on earth, the king of the gods strings up the queen of the gods and delivers a lecture on power. As Hera describes it, Zeus's treatment is ungodly. I marked the page so I could read it repeatedly.

On the quadrangles and in the classrooms, however, my twisted lust went largely unsatisfied.

Once, at a costume party in the architecture college, I saw a student with white cords around her ankles. She was wearing black tights, which made the ligatures stand out. But her legwear wasn't important. What was important was that her ankles were one knot away from being cinched. She was one step away from having to hobble or hop.

I was convinced that this student had rope in her heart, that she was majoring in strictural mechanics, that she had crafted a masochistic mockup, that she was drafting a dungeon blueprint.

I was sure that this person and I could build something together. We could interface in a torturous environment. But I was not feeling knotty enough to approach her. Even though I was wearing a cowboy costume, I lacked the lariat to lasso anyone on the hoof.

Weeks passed without sightings of string.

I scanned the local newspaper for reports of deviant incidents, and lucked onto an account of a sorority initiation. A new sister had been tied hand and foot, driven to the countryside, and dropped off. She had to find her own way back to the sorority house, where she was dressed down and given the pan-Hellenic pledge. I memorized the article, then hit the roads, looking for lost sisters.

All I saw was a woman getting arrested. She was standing next to a police cruiser, wearing sex-enforcement bracelets. I stared at her until the cops threatened to take me in for peeping.

Several ropeless months passed. Then my fortune turned. I met a student who told me that her former boyfriend was skilled at tickling. He would move in, grab her above the waist, engineer a fall, and give her the twitching treatment. During the finger torture, she would blubber, or worse, she would screech, or even worse, she would pee.

"There I was," she said, "not knowing anything about laughter or tears, yet aware, as Heidegger wrote, that knowing does not consist in mere information or notions about something."

I wanted to deconstruct giggling, to calculate the meaning of cackling. I wanted to examine tickling theory, then advance to tickling praxis. I wanted to leave the realm of philosophy and enter the world of idiocy. I wanted to become a phenomenological cowboy and make my new friend whinny.

"Why don't you take off your shoes?" I asked.

When I had a target for my frenzied fingers, I trapped her legs with one arm, flexed my free fingers next to her tootsies, and struck.

She kicked at me and moved away.

I went for her ribs with my hands, snapping my digits like piranhas' jaws. I found the T-spot beneath her lowest rib, went shoulder-to-shoulder with her, and held on for dear laugh.

She screamed, "Ta!" and elbowed me.

"What's wrong?" I gasped.

"You don't fit my idea of a transcendental tickler," she said. "You're just not a comical hermeneutical hero."

She walked out without so much as a snort.

Defeated, I went to the deepest part of the library stacks and zeroed in on the history of hysteria. I boned up on ostrich feathers, horsehair dusters, wood-ball massagers and fur mufflers. I read about grazing navels, rubbing rib cages, tweaking nipples and pricking feet. I wanted to become a tee-hee expert, a hee-haw master, a guffaw guru.

I wanted to find a partner who would appreciate a little pinch and dandle, who would giggle till she cried, who would shriek till she peed, who would never say, "Uncle!"

I realized that I would have to change my routine. I would have to buy a pair of hand-exercise devices, those plier-like graspers with springs. I would have to strengthen my digits through countless repetitions. When my hands became sinewy and massive, I would be able to get a grip on funny sex.

*

OFF WITH A HITCH

My first long hitch was from upstate New York to the middle of Ohio. I wanted to travel—by any mode necessary—to see a young woman I'd met about a year earlier.

The first driver who stopped for me was a woman who said she was going to Cortland, and I thought, Wow, Cortland, that's a long way!

But it turned out she was going only to Cortland Street, so I stepped out a few blocks from where I'd started.

It took me about three hours to get to an interstate highway. At one point, while I stood on someone's front lawn, a woman drove by and shot at me with her thumb and forefinger.

On the expressway, my journey went faster. Even so, I spent a few hours on the berm, sitting on my backpack on the gravel. While sitting there, I made up a koan: "It is kind of hard to travel, on gravel."

While chanting my koan, I saw a police car pull up. "Take your hands out of your pockets!" an officer said through a bullhorn.

When I didn't respond immediately, two officers charged toward me. "Put your luggage on the ground," they yelled, "and step back!"

I complied with their request.

After they'd searched through my belongings, they told me to go down a nearby ramp, walk outside the toll gate, and wait.

Next to the tollbooths, I got rid of some illegal-looking pills that had mysteriously appeared in my backpack.

Eventually, a tractor trailer stopped for me. As I climbed into the cab, I noticed a look of disappointment on the driver's face and realized he'd mistaken me for a woman.

"I've been waiting outside a long time," I said.

"Okay," he said. "You can ride in the bunk."

I climbed onto the platform behind his head, and he fired up a tiny pipe. After he'd smoked, he swallowed some pills. "With the right mix of speed and weed," he said, "I can sit behind this wheel for twenty hours."

When a truck with "Roadway" lettered on its side rolled past, my driver said, "Those trucks are called 'Roadway' because they're always on the road, and they're always in the way."

After dark, he let me off in eastern Ohio. After a while, a rusted station wagon stopped for me. When I got in, the driver asked where I was coming from.

"Ithaca," I said.

"Attica?" he asked. "Maximum security, right? I have friends there."

When I arrived in central Ohio, my woman friend told me I couldn't stay with her, but I could stay with some people she knew.

I spent the night in an apartment filled with university students. One of them was a man who used a cane when he walked. "When I got shot in Vietnam," he told me, "I didn't know I was hit. I thought I'd tripped over a root. Later, I found out the bullet went through my stomach."

He pulled his cane apart and revealed a foot-long knife blade.

The next morning, my woman friend came to visit me. She took me to the nearby campus, and we walked around the grass Oval.

"Is this all we're going to do?" I asked.

"What do you mean?" she said.

"I thought we'd be more than friends."

"Really?" she asked. "All my old boyfriends just want to be friends when they visit."

At that point, I thought I might take a bus home, but then I realized I couldn't afford a ticket. So I hit the road on foot.

*

Another time, I hitchhiked to Iowa, because I knew a different young woman there.

When I phoned her with my plan, she discouraged me, but somehow I didn't understand her message.

On the Chicago beltway, I got caught in a steady rain. I walked into a service-area restaurant, found the truckers' section and begged for a ride, but no one answered my plea.

I walked out to the pavement, dropped to my knees, put my hands together and prayed. Shortly, a police car stopped. "You can't conduct a church service on the road," an officer said.

In Quad Cities, I walked along the highway in a snowstorm.

When I arrived at my friend's dorm, she was away from her room, so I sat in a hallway and listened to some women students talk. "You have to watch out for men," one of them said.

Noticing me, she hissed, "There's one now!"

At one point, a gang of men with shaved heads ran through the hallway. They were making animal sounds and carrying the legs of a disassembled pool table.

I slept in the dorm lounge. Early on, I spotted an object that looked like an old hot dog lying on the floor. I was hungry, but I didn't touch the meat. Occasionally, my friend brought me food she had stolen from the cafeteria. All during my visit, the hot dog stayed in the same spot.

On my last night there, she allowed me to share her bed, but she wouldn't allow me to touch her. So I stayed on my side of the mattress.

In the morning, she asked, "Did you have a wet dream?"

"Why do you ask?" I said.

"The sheet is wet," she said.

I looked at the place I'd occupied and saw a sizable damp patch.

*

In the summer, I hitchhiked north. Along the way, a woman in a bikini stopped for me. I thought this was unusual, but I didn't ask about the beachwear. Instead, I took a nap. A couple of hours later, my nearly naked driver discharged me.

Near the Canadian border, I met a college friend, and we continued on together.

At one point, a sports car stopped for us, and the driver said, "I can take one of you, but not both."

"We can sit on each other's lap," my friend said.

We rode that way, one on top of the other, for many miles.

Another time, we waited by the side of the road for more than four hours, watching rush-hour traffic go by. When a car pulled out of the stream and stopped, we ran up to it. A woman inside said, "I'm not giving you a ride. I'm just lost."

We helped her read a road map, then went back to hitching.

Shortly, we got a ride with a man who spoke only French. He gave us two yellow pills, and we swallowed them. We ended up on the gravel shoulder, waiting for something psychotropic to happen, but all we felt was drowsiness. We decided the pills were antihistamines.

Later, two women gave us a ride. They brought us to the Saint Lawrence River and parked. On the riverbank, they shared some Red Lebanese hashish.

Another day, we met a young man who wanted to travel with us. Between rides, he walked into convenience stores and slipped packages of lunch meat down the front of his overalls. In a youth hostel, he dismantled a water faucet to make a hash pipe. When I asked if he'd ever gone fishing in Canada, he said, "I have a rod, but I keep it in my pants."

In another hostel, I saw the same two women who had taken us to the river. From my cot, I could see their sleeping bags rising and falling. I walked past them a couple of times, but they didn't acknowledge me.

I didn't know my friend was gay until we got back from our trip. I walked into his house and saw him kissing another man. But I might have been mistaken. He might have been kissing a woman who had short hair.

Either way, he never forgave me. Whenever he saw me with a woman, he would ask, "Why do you always walk ahead of her? Why don't you listen to her? Why are you always at the wheel when you're riding in a car with her? Why do you act like a typical man? Where are your politics?"

I had no answers for these questions.

*

UNREAL CITY

I was walking around the business district, the commercial district, along with throngs of shoppers—people carrying bags with handles, people who were serious about making purchases—but I was totally broke. I mean, I had a place to stay and I would be able to get back home—but I didn't have two coins to rub together in my pocket.

That was okay, because I was passing display windows, and I could appreciate the stacks of things. Once, I stopped to look at earflap hats, navy-wool coats and hiking boots—all sorts of outdoor clothes—and felt that I was not in a city, but at a campsite.

I kept walking and saw vacation posters, electronic equipment, eyeglasses, greeting cards, salads, draft beer labels, khakis, sweaters, suitcases on wheels, books, art materials and office supplies.

I was sad, because I couldn't go on a spree, I couldn't load up with goods. But I was also happy, because in a way I was free, even though nothing I saw was free.

Well, I guessed, if I threw a heavy object through one of the windows, some things would be free. But then I would no longer be shopping; I'd be looting.

*

I quickly learned that I was the only Twinkie—the only Asian halfie—among the people I encountered. I couldn't fool anyone except myself that, as a half-white, half-yellow person, I was passing in my new society. So I looked for others, like Bumblebees—black-and-yellow halfies—who resembled Twinkies, at least in terms of racial percentage. But I couldn't find any, and when I asked where to look, people said, "What are you, F.O.B.?"

"I may be naive," I said, "but I'm not fresh off the boat."

I kept looking for other mutts, but met only an occasional angry dog accompanying an official guard. I didn't want those mongrels sicced on me.

*

I was walking down the street wearing a lei—not an everyday accessory, but I'd just been to a Hawaiian restaurant—when a hooligan approached me and asked, "Where's the luau?"

"I've got a luau," I said, "but I keep it in my pants."

I noticed a black blur as a beer can came flying through the air. Then *crack!* I got hit on the head. At first, I couldn't think—a tingling ran from my skull to my toes. But as soon as my brain started working again, I thanked the tiki of hops that it was a can, not a bottle. It was a can, not a keg. A can, not a truck. Still, it was a full can, and it packed a punch.

I picked up the can—it was no longer a black blur; it was more of a silver cylinder. And then I went looking for the bloody haole idiot who threw it. When I found this idiot, I was sure, we would hoist a few. But we wouldn't be hoisting beers.

*

I was standing on a corner, in desperate need of transportation, and rain was falling. Fortunately, I had a hat, with a long bill—if "bill" was the word to describe the flat, curved projection that looked like a duck's beak. I was a standing duck, with one wing flapping, waving at yellow cabs, cars the color of real ducks' bills, though my bill, the bill of my hat, was black.

My hat matched my mood, which was also dark—a result of waving my wing at indifferent drivers while getting spritzed, then drenched. I was flapping without flying in the midst of a continuous—sometimes softer, sometimes harder—spitting, pelting, drilling rain.

*

I lost something essential when the collision occurred. I lost it when the impact scared the bejesus out of me.

I was walking across several lanes of traffic when I felt the contact of a car against my person and the meeting of my body with the pavement. I was so scared I didn't have time to pray or curse, to shout, "What the dickens!" or "What the deuce!"

Aside from the absence of my sweet bejesus, I was fine. I still had the living daylights. I could still dance with the devil. I just didn't have a personal relationship with the ineffable power anymore. I was staring into bloody hell, and I needed to rekindle my faith.

*

INNER-CITY BLUES

In the morning, I walked out of my building and saw my upstairs neighbor on the street. When I looked closely, I noticed that he was wearing an alarm clock around his neck. The timepiece was hanging by its electrical cord, and the wire was knotted behind his head. I also saw that he wasn't wearing shoes.

When he saw me, he asked, "What's the big megillah?"

I wanted to ask him why the neckwear was necessary and shoes were not. I wanted to give him money or my phone number, or just throw a butterfly net over his head. But the clock necklace reminded me that I was late for work, so I said, "Never mind," and kept on my way. As I passed out of reach, I regretted that I had done nothing.

*

When I got to the office, I was called into a meeting in a conference room. Two new bosses were there, along with other people from my department. One of the new bosses did most of the talking, while the other mainly laughed.

"We're taking over," the first boss said, "but it's not political."

"Actually, it is political," the second said, giggling.

"Does anyone have any questions?" the first asked.

"May I stay with the company?" a staffer asked.

"You can stay, but you can't work on the product anymore. You can work on promotions."

"I'm ready to sell," the staffer said.

"I know most of you are ambitious," the first boss said, "but some of you aren't." He looked at me and said, "For example... " then said my name.

"That's a good one," the second boss said, holding his jiggling stomach.

"We don't plan to make any changes," the first boss said, "at least for the rest of the day."

The second boss slapped the conference table and snorted.

*

When the first boss asked me to come to his office, I was sure I had reached the end of my tenure with the company.

"Have a seat," he said.

I took a comfortable chair, and he continued, "As you know, we've been making some changes around here."

At that moment, a young woman walked into the office. "I'm here for my appointment," she announced. "I've looked at our latest project, and I'm ready to discuss it."

Since I had nothing to contribute, the boss told me I could leave. Either that, or I just sneaked out of the room. The new honcho didn't fire me; he just never spoke to me again.

*

In the evening, I went to a drawing class in a basement studio. The place was filled with people at easels, and it smelled of cats.

I set out my art supplies, opened my paper tablet and stared at a model standing on a platform. She had hair that stuck straight out. When I was finished sketching, I saw that I'd made her head look like a flying saucer.

During a break, I walked out of the studio to escape the cat spray. On the stairs, several artists were smoking. A young woman was sitting there with a drawing book.

"I know the studio owner," she told me, "and I like cats."

"I like life drawing," I said, "but I'm not a nudist."

"Then you won't be arrested for exposing yourself tonight," she said.

When I went back into the studio, I switched from charcoal to Conte crayon, but I could not improve my rendering of the model's hair as an unidentified flying object.

*

On my way home, I stopped at a pizza storefront and asked for a couple of slices. I sat at a counter next to a large window, so I could watch people crossing an intersection outside. One person, a young man wearing a T-shirt and baggy pants, caught my eye and came in.

He looked my plate. "Do you want your crusts?" he asked.

"No," I said.

He picked up a stick of burnt dough that had some tomato sauce on it and began to chew. "I love crusts," he said.

I ate most of my second slice, trying not to gnaw too close to the outside strip, then slid the leftover part to him.

*

When I got home, I saw water pouring through the ceiling of my apartment. I ran upstairs, found the door to my neighbor's apartment open, and went in. I saw my neighbor cowering in a corner. He wasn't wearing any clothes, but he still had the alarm clock around his neck. Water was pouring from all of the faucets in his place.

"Are you crazy?" I asked.

"As a loon," he said.

I turned off the faucets and went back downstairs. I called our landlord and reported the flood.

Shortly, some officials arrived to remove my neighbor. As they led him out of the building, I saw that they had got him dressed, but they hadn't been able to find his shoes.

*

I called the woman I'd spoken with at the drawing class, and she said she would meet me at a bar.

When I arrived, I found her sitting at a table with about six other people. There wasn't a free chair next to her, so I talked with her friends.

After a while, all of us left the bar. The friends scattered, but my new friend said she would take me to a restaurant opening party.

At the door to the restaurant, she told me I would have to wait outside.

"Why can't I come in with you?" I asked.

"Because the people here won't think you're cool," she said.

She went inside, and I stood on the sidewalk. After waiting a long time, I gave up and went home.

*

A couple of weeks later, she called me. She seemed surprised that I hadn't called. I didn't tell her that my silence had been deliberate, and so we arranged to meet at her apartment.

When I got there, she showed me her stereo system and a closet full of coats. "These are all gifts," she said.

"Who gave them to you?" I asked.

"A doctor," she said. "He also wanted to give me a home Pap smear. He said it would involve only a small instrument and wouldn't hurt, but I said no."

We walked to a nearby place for dinner.

At a table, she said, "I don't care about money, but other women do. They're going to ask how much you make. Fifty thousand? Forty thousand? Thirty thousand?"

"You're right," I said.

"You're going to have trouble," she added, "finding a partner who's biracial, like you. Isn't there an organization where you can register to buy an Asian wife?"

I bought dinner for both of us.

Afterward, we walked across town to my apartment. Inside, I showed her a hook in the ceiling over my bed. Then I showed her a dartboard on the wall. "How about we play a game?" I asked. "If I win, I get to attach you to the hook. If you win, I don't."

"What if we don't, and say we did?" she said.

Later, we went to bed. Before we got in, she took off her underwear and put it into a plastic bag. "If you touch me," she said, "I'll freak."

We fell asleep, but I woke shortly after. Seeing my bedmate unconscious, I felt somewhat bolder, but not brave enough to wake her.

*

I called her later, but she didn't seem happy to hear from me. When I asked if she wanted to meet again, she said, "Maybe in a year or so."

"Why so long?" I asked.

"You have a hook in your ceiling!" she said.

That, I supposed, explained everything.

*

Early in the morning, I looked out my window and saw men from the next-door noodle factory taking a break. Three of them were sitting on the curb, eating from bowls with chopsticks. Another was sleeping face-down on the sidewalk. They were wearing white uniforms, and their skin and hair were powdered with flour.

One of the seated men was feeding pigeons bits of his food. The birds were strutting back and forth in front of him; now and then, one would perch on his folded legs. The man was throwing rice grains with his chopsticks.

A cat crept up behind the man and watched the pigeons, stalking them. When the birds realized they were in danger, they took flight in unison and veered away.

*

RUBBED THE WRONG WAY

She often lied to her mother so she could spend the night with me. She would call her mother from my place and say she was staying with a woman friend.

After she made the call, we would go straight to my bed. There, we would engage in my own brand of intimacy. Sometimes I would hold her hands, and sometimes we would kiss, but most times I just rubbed against her.

After a long period of frottage, she would tell me that her thighs were sore and that she could feel shooting pains. At that point, I would stop rubbing, and we would have normal, vanilla sex.

After several months of such encounters, she moved in with me.

*

She didn't work regularly when we lived together. She took temporary jobs or held full-time positions that lasted only until she was dismissed.

I paid for her to take a typing course. The course was only three days long, but she didn't finish it.

We agreed that she would contribute a hundred dollars a month for living expenses. She did this once, then borrowed the money back before the end of the month.

She found where I kept paper cash in a book, and sometimes she took twenties.

Eventually, I stopped asking her for the hundred at the beginning of the month. I just paid the rent and the phone and utility bills myself.

*

At night, she smoked cigarettes and I smoked marijuana.
One time, I said, "I think all forms of life are related."
"We're all carbon-based," she replied.

"One creature has use for another," I said, "somehow or other. The creature I have no use for may have use for me, and vice versa."

"You mean," she asked, "that everything is linked? That's called the food chain, dear."

"Yes," I said, "and the perception of our relation is like the awareness of self."

"That sounds Freudian," she said.

"Maybe it's Jungian," I said, "or an anima/animus thing."

"We're all animals," she said.

"I'm not talking Darwin," I replied. "That's natural selection."

"I think you're a good creature," she said. "But the good part is hidden so deeply I can't see it."

*

She often was seriously ill. She complained of chronic inflammation, and once she went to the hospital for a radiological test of her digestive tract. Another time, she tripped on a curb while crossing a street and had to have knee surgery.

"You would have liked the operation," she told me afterward, "because the doctors tied me up."

"How did they do that?" I asked.

"They taped my thumbs to my shoulders. That way, in case I woke up while they were operating, I couldn't push their hands away."

*

On a holiday, I went with her to visit her parents.

As I sat on a couch in their living room, I inhaled and exhaled loudly, through my mouth, because my sinuses were blocked.

"Can you breathe?" her mother asked me.

"Yes," I said. "I'm just asthmatic."

"He's just repressed," my girlfriend said.

I shut my mouth and tried to breathe quietly, through my nostrils, like everyone else.

*

Another time, after we'd engaged yet again in my own brand of sex, she took me to a party.

Coincidentally, a former boyfriend of hers was at the same gathering. He was a large Caucasian, sitting on a couch. "He works for a book publisher," my girlfriend told me.

Cockily, I sat next to him. He turned to me and said, "When you're wearing tight jeans and you spread your knees, you can show off your mound."

He moved his legs apart and cupped one of his hands over his crotch. I could see a definite bulge there.

When the talk shifted to occupation, I said, "You know, I do fiction writing."

"Oh," he said. "I want to sell books, not shred them."

My girlfriend sat across from him and propped one leg over the other. She was wearing translucent stockings, and marks from our esoteric sex episode were visible around her ankles.

Her former boyfriend stared at the marks and said, "My God!"

*

Once, in the bedroom, she asked me to try on her underwear. I didn't want to do it, but she had a pair of panties ready, so I took them, stepped out of my briefs, and stepped in. The fabric was thin and slippery, and the garment naturally had no front opening. I had the sensation of being squeezed in, shrunken, unmanned.

"How do they feel?" she asked.

"Tight," I said, "but smooth."

"Maybe you should put on my slip," she said, "and some of my makeup."

When she was finished with me, I looked prettier than ever.

*

One day, soon after another strange sex session, she went for a routine doctor visit. When she got home, she told me that a nurse had seen hickeys on her buttocks and had given her a scolding.

"Where did those bruises come from?" the nurse had asked.

"My boyfriend," she'd said.

"I'm giving you a phone number," the nurse had said. "You can call it anytime, and you don't have to give your name.

Someone will always be there to talk to you about domestic abuse."

*

I deviously fashioned a weird sex device around a plumbing pipe near the ceiling of my bedroom. I constructed a hoisting system, complete with pulley, anchor and cleat. Then I asked my girlfriend to try it out. "You can trust me," I said, "it won't hurt."

"Yes, it will," she said.

"If you let me do it," I said, "I'll give you something."

"Like what?" she asked.

"Flowers? Ice cream?"

"I get those things anyway," she said.

Eventually, she relented and allowed me to attach her to my unusual instrument. Once she was all fixed up, I started rubbing against her. The rubbing didn't last long, though, because she looked at me and said, "You're a sick puppy!"

*

One night, she told me she was going to stay with a girlfriend. She called me from the girlfriend's apartment to let me know she had arrived safely.

When she came back the next morning, she said she had stayed with a man.

"You weren't at your friend's place?" I asked.

"No," she said. "I called from the man's apartment."

"Did you have sex with him?" I asked.

"Of course," she said.

"How many times?"

"Who was counting?"

I didn't sleep that night, but I went to work the next morning. To my surprise, I found that I could do my job almost as well as I could have if I had slept.

*

Before she moved out, she asked me to give her half of the money I had in the bank.

"Why?" I asked.

"As a separation settlement," she said.

I didn't have much money, but I did the math and split what was in my savings account. I made a withdrawal and wrote her a check.

*

When she left, I helped her move. I cheerfully carried her belongings out of my apartment and into a van. Then I rode to her new place, which was in a neighborhood more upscale than mine, and helped her unload. I wasn't upset. In fact, I was in good spirits.

Inside her new apartment, I saw strange furniture. Apparently, she had spent part of the money I had given her on interior decorations. A couple of the pieces—a couch and a reclining chair—looked much more comfortable than anything I owned.

*

PECULIAR NEEDS

In the wake of being cheated on (overtly) after a span of monogamy, I decided it was time to skip out, at least temporarily. Fortunately, someone came along to make my own infidelity easy, someone I knew but hadn't heard from in a long time, someone who had been enjoying (or avoiding) domestic bliss herself. Anyway, she called and told me the bad (actually good) news about her finished marriage, and I said, "Let's get together immediately."

*

At dinner, I asked if she wanted to play Cowboys and Indians.

"You mean with weapons?" she asked.

"Weapons?" I asked.

"You know, guns and tomahawks."

"No," I said, "I don't own any weapons. I mean with household implements, like clothesline and clothespins. You'll be the white settler, and I'll be the angry native American."

"We've been through this before," she said. "Don't bring that up again."

"Do you think I'm sick?"

"You mean crazy?" she asked. "I think you're a fetishist, but you're harmless. You might even grow out of it."

"I doubt it," I said.

"Okay," she said. "Tonight, I will make myself available to your peculiar needs."

*

After we left the restaurant, we went to a discount store. We walked through aisles full of packaged goods, beneath blinding fluorescent lights. I wanted to buy rope, but strangely, amid the headache remedies, candles and cleaning supplies, I could not find anything that could be used for rigging, not even sash cord. All I saw was kite string, and what could I do with that? Tie fingers and toes?

Not far from the discount mart, we found a sex-novelty store and went in. Among the edible underwear and genital-shaped cookies, I spotted handcuffs. Even though the implements were poorly welded and looked like they might crack apart at their seams, I bought not one pair but two.

*

At my friend's suggestion, we made our way to her new place. Once there, I felt nervous. "What if your roommate comes home?" I asked.

"I guess I'll make coffee for us in shackles."

I took out my newly purchased gear. "First," I said, "we have to have some rules."

"Like what?"

"Like you have to call me Sir."

I could see she was about to laugh, but she said, "Okay ... Sir."

"Also, we need a code word, in case what I do gets too intense. We need a word that means 'Stop.' Okay?"

"Like what?"

" 'Computer.' "

"Okay, 'computer.' "

"Don't say it yet!"

"Of course not, Sir."

"Please," I said, "don't say anything at all."

I took one of her wrists and clicked on one of the bracelets, then grasped her free wrist and fastened the other, matching circlet.

I removed her shoes and socks, expecting to hear the code word, but didn't hear anything.

I took one of her ankles, locked on an as-yet-unused bracelet, bent her knees so her heels were touching her fingers behind her back, wrapped the ankle chain around the wrist chain, and snapped on the other anklet.

I turned on her television and watched some news. She flexed her hands and feet and rolled from side to side.

"Do you know what this is called?" I asked.

"Am I allowed to talk, Sir?"

"Yes."

"Is it called kinky?"

"No, it's called a hogtie."

"A hogtie! How unflattering! Am I just a piece of bacon to you?"

"Of course not," I lied.

"Okay, Sir," she said, "now that you've had your fantasy, what are you going to do?"

"I'm going to watch TV."

"You mean this is it? Where's the action?"

I understood then that we were supposed to go beyond bondage *qua* restraint. I was supposed to bind her and bang her, rope her and ream her, pin her and poke her, tie her and tool her, cuff her and coit her, hoist her and hose her, leash her and lick her, web her and whip her, tape her and tickle her, string her up and stroke her, restrain her and ravish her, dangle her and defile her, fasten her and finger her, pillory her and penetrate her, thumbscrew her and screw her, and fetter her and fuck her.

"Lots of times, nothing happens," I said.

"Why do you have to do this?" she asked.

"I think it's connected with my relationship with my father. I had no control when I was a child."

"You had a bad childhood, so you have to immobilize me? You were mistreated, so you have to humiliate me?"

"That's it!"

"Is this what I get for my infractions? I forget to make my bed, and I get restrained? I go to work late, so I have to lose circulation in my hands and feet?"

She buried her face in the pillow. At first, I thought she was crying, but when I looked again I saw she was laughing.

"I'll let you go before tomorrow," I said.

"You take yourself way too seriously," she said.

"This is no game," I said. "What would you do if someone found you like this?"

"I'd ask them to join us for tea and B&D."

At that point, I remembered the code word. "I give up," I said. "*Computer!*"

*

On my way home, I became convinced that I had left my apartment keys at her place and that I would have to return to retrieve them.

I also had the feeling that my underwear was on backwards. Worse, I wasn't wearing ordinary Skivvies; I had a wood frame strapped to my pelvis. My only consolation was the knowledge that I was not the only person saddled with such a rigid undergarment. Many of the people around me were wearing the same contraption. We would all have to undergo further training in order to use our new prosthesis.

*

NIGHT SHIFT

When I got to my office, the room was bare. There was a computer on the floor—no desk, no furniture.

I ignored the lack of equipment and started to work on a project. I asked a co-worker about the routine I was learning, then realized I'd asked the wrong person. I'd asked someone who was going to be dismissed from the company soon.

My task was to help a contestant in a survival game. This man was going to try to stay alive in the wilderness for three days, with the help of only his cat. No one knew exactly what the cat would do, but everyone understood that the animal was a better hunter, runner and climber than the man, and the animal was smarter than anyone guessed. My assignment was to keep the cat healthy until the game started—I would be a cat-sitter. But I doubted I could complete the task. I knew I wasn't a very good caregiver.

I saw that another colleague had started working on the same project. Since the cat required the attention of only one person, there was nothing left for me to do.

On this day, I couldn't verbally convince people to accept my opinion, but I could wrestle with them to get my point across. A rubber mat had been laid down in a file room for this purpose.

I got on the mat with a man who was much bigger than I was. I put him in a headlock—I trapped his neck in the crook of my elbow. He gasped for air and his face turned red. I knew that he would soon understand what I was trying to say.

After the wrestling match, I looked disheveled. The hair on my head stuck up in waves.

I went into the men's room, stood in front of a mirror, and hacked at my hair. I couldn't see the back of my head, so I concentrated on the front and sides. I wanted my colleagues to notice a difference when I returned.

I chopped deliberately, sawing for a feathery effect. Occasionally, someone would come in; sometimes that person would use a nearby sink. I had to work fast, because I didn't want to be questioned or stopped.

Later, the people in my department were called into a meeting, but I was not invited. When the staffers emerged from their conference, they had ties and belts around their necks, as if they were about to be strangled or were about to strangle themselves. They hugged each other in farewell gestures, but most of them didn't come to me for comfort.

One man put his head in my arms and cried, but he wouldn't tell me why he was sad. I couldn't remember who he was or where I'd met him. Maybe we'd met at the beach.

A second meeting was held, and I was asked to attend. Everyone took a seat at a big table. My boss sat next to me and started to chuckle. He was paging through a book full of fetish images. He handed me the book and said, "This is your cup of tea. Pass it around."

The pictures in the book embarrassed me. I didn't want to touch the pages.

The boss said he was giving me a new assignment. "I want you to blow things up," he said. "You don't have to blow yourself up. You just have to attach bombs to buses and run away."

"I can't do it," I said.

He got up and started to leave the room.

"Should I come with you?" I asked.

"No," he said, and I understood then that my tenure at the firm had ended.

I decided to turn my boss in to the authorities, even though I knew that doing so would not get my job back.

I was given a pill to take. My co-workers were given the same pill. The medicine turned out to be cyanide, but luckily I didn't swallow it. I saw one of my colleagues take his pill and die.

*

ISLANDS

Just before we were scheduled to leave for vacation, she took her travel ticket away from me. She said she didn't want me to hold the ticket, even though I'd purchased it.

"Okay," I said, "you keep the ticket. But why don't you stay at my place overnight? That way, we can start our trip together in the morning."

"I'll stay at my place," she said.

I knew that, since she never allowed me to visit her place, the two of us would be spending the night alone, but I asked anyway, "Can I stay with you at your place?"

"Of course not," she said.

"Okay," I said, "but how about we talk on the phone during the evening?"

That won't be necessary," she said.

I called her anyway. "I think you should come over," I said.

"I have other things to do," she said.

"Well, tell me when you'll come over," I said. "Give me a date."

"If you're giving me orders," she said, "we may as well break up now."

"I'm not giving orders. I just want to talk. I don't want to break up."

"You aren't listening to me," she said. "You never listen to me! That's the problem."

"I'm listening," I said. "I heard you. But I think you're not listening to me."

"That does it," she said. "It's over."

I heard a dead silence that indicated she had hung up her phone. I tried calling back, but got only a ringing that meant she had unplugged her patch cord.

All I wanted to do was act out. I didn't want to relate to anyone. I didn't want to interact, to be polite. I was sociopathic, and I knew it.

I wanted to escape. I wanted to have fun. But there was no fun to be had anywhere.

I had sworn off drugs—I'd split from spliff. I had promised myself I would not get high to feel love. I would find other things to love, things like sunsets and flowers and bees. But there was nothing remotely resembling any of these within my reach. I lived in the inner city. I had to leave my apartment, walk through someone else's living space, and cross the hall to go to the bathroom. Unless all I had to do was number one, in which case I could step out to the fire escape.

I wanted to get out. I needed to move around. But taking a walk was out of the question, because my immediate vicinity smelled like fish. I was living next to the biggest open-air fish market in the city.

So I decided to clean up my place. Cleanliness, after all, was next to godliness. I started by reordering things, aligning bedcovers, alphabetizing books. I threw out papers, starting with the ones that were most recent, then going back five, ten years. I felt most satisfied when I sent the old material to the shredder. I wanted to have empty rooms, no belongings. If I moved, I wanted to travel light. If I died, I wanted nothing embarrassing left behind.

But I wanted to get beneath the surfaces. I didn't care about smudges or dust bunnies. I wanted to get at the drains. So I took a container of sulfuric acid, unscrewed the top, and began to pour. I must have been nervous, because I dropped the bottle and globules of acid splashed up and hit me. Small drops stuck to my fingers, forearms and a lower eyelid. A big glob hit my thigh. When I peeled off my pants, I saw that the skin was brown and bubbling. There was no blood, but there was a lot of oozing and stinging.

*

In the morning, I went to an airport to meet my girlfriend. She was wearing hiking clothes, with boots and a belt pack. Her eye irises looked pale, and her pupils were slitted in an odd way; they reminded me of the nickname I'd given her: Snake.

"Why are you limping?" she asked.

"I had a cleaning accident," I said.

She told me she had changed her seat assignment so she wouldn't have to sit next to me. "You can change your seat, too," she said, "if you want to talk with me."

"But if you hadn't changed your seat," I said, "we'd be sitting next to each other anyway."

"If I hadn't changed my seat," she repeated, mimicking me, "I'd have to listen to your harassment."

"I'm not harassing you," I said. "I'm just asking you."

"You want only one thing," she said. Then, raising her voice, she informed everyone in the waiting area. "He wants only one thing!"

"Why don't you switch back to your original seat?" I begged.

"I'm not changing again," she said.

On our way through a security checkpoint, I saw a poster showing things not permitted in the passenger area of a plane. There were diagrams of scissors, nail clippers, a Swiss army knife, and an old-fashioned, ball-shaped bomb with a fuse on top. I promised myself that, if asked, I would say nothing like "I have a bomb in my bag."

The Snake must have complained about me, because before we got on the plane, a uniformed guard took me aside. "If you disrupt the flight," he said, "the pilot will turn the plane around, and you'll be arrested when the plane lands."

During the flight, I sat in my original seat, and she sat in her new seat. I couldn't see her from where I was sitting, so I spent my time watching data readouts of altitude, outside temperature, time to destination, and air and ground speed. Did the readings in minus degrees have anything to do with the lack of oxygen, I wondered. How high would we have to go before we were in outer space? Why were air speed and ground speed different? Was a plane more like a ship, which proceeded in knots? Were my thoughts all tangled up because I didn't want to admit I was getting rejected, or what?

As soon as we arrived at our island destination, she told me she wanted to return home.

"How can you do that?" I said. "We have reservations for a flight back."

"I'll call the airline and change the date."

"You can't to that," I stated feebly.

"Of course I can," she said.

And just as she'd done with her seat, she booked a new flight. She didn't even have to leave the airport before getting on a plane headed for home.

As I walked along a ramp to the outside of the terminal, I was greeted by a woman who was nearly topless. She turned out, though, to be wearing multiple flower necklaces. She was my welcoming committee. She took off one of the necklaces and put it over my head. Then she took my picture with an instant camera and gave me the print. "Have you ever gotten lei-ed?" she asked.

"Splash me again," I said. "I didn't catch your wave."

"You know what I mean, Captain," she said.

*

BEFORE THE MOVE

When she came to visit, she stood at the entranceway, folded her arms, and eyed my apartment suspiciously, as if scanning for evidence of self-abuse. We talked, watched some television, and went up to the roof to look at the orange-tinged sky. Then we came back inside and had sex.

Our session was as intense as I could get away with, or as intense as I could devise before feeling guilty. Afterward, she left the room and went to the bathroom. When she returned, she said, "The well is dry."

"What do you mean?" I asked.

"You've been dipping in your reservoir," she said, "draining your wineskin, tapping your tree."

"No way!" I lied.

*

Once, when she was happy with me, she made a sculpture of her body. When I wasn't home, she installed it in my apartment.

I came home and found a pair of leg tights and a shirt sewn together and stuffed with cloth. The effigy was hanging by its ankles from the ceiling of my bedroom.

Another time, when she was unhappy, she stacked my pornographic videos on my eating table and left a note. "This is what I meant!" it read. "You don't even bother to hide them!"

*

She changed her hair. First, she dyed it black, blacker than my hair.

Then she started to cut it. She sported successively shorter styles, until all she had was about a half-inch of hair on the top of her head.

One time, when we were traveling by car, we stopped at a rest area. She went into the women's room, and when she came out she said, "I frightened a little girl in there."

"How?" I asked.

"The girl saw me and started to run. But her mother told her it was okay, I wasn't a man."

*

I threw away all of my videos and sexual paraphernalia. I made a bundle of films and leather goods and placed it in a wire basket on the sidewalk. Then I crossed the street and watched.

After a while, a muscular man looked into the garbage basket and pulled out a riding crop. He slapped it against his palm, then walked away with it.

I went home bereft.

*

She said the only place she would see me was at her office, so I went there on a Saturday afternoon.

I found her in the one cubicle that was lit. She was sitting at a desk, sorting papers into three-ring binders.

I wanted physical contact, so I stood behind her and touched her shoulder. She turned, then went back to work.

"All my boss does," she said, "is play video games. He gives me instructions while jiggling his joystick. He expects me to make sense of his code."

"Why don't we leave here together?" I asked.

"Not today," she said. "Maybe someday, if you keep coming back for a few months."

She continued to put papers into folder pockets, so I walked out alone.

*

My apartment had no heat, so at night I pulled a knit hat over my ears, wrapped a wool scarf around my neck, and covered my body with blankets. I left a hole in my wrappings so I could breathe. After a few hours, I thought I was suffocating, yet my nose felt frostbitten.

In the morning, I ripped off the hat, scarf and blankets and ran out of my bedroom.

*

The next time I talked to her, I told her I had a cold.

She brought a bulb of garlic to my apartment.

"If you eat this, you'll get better," she said.

She separated and peeled the cloves, then poured oil into a pan. She seared the nuggets on my stove.

She slid the blackened bits onto a plate and said, "You have to eat all of them."

Each piece was bitter on the outside and spicy on the inside. Halfway through the helping, I felt I couldn't eat another bite.

"Will part of a dose cure me?" I asked.

"No," she said.

I somehow downed the entire bulb. Then I waited for a miracle to occur.

A couple of days later, I was still sick as a dog.

*

I asked if I could come to her apartment.

"There is a leak in my place," she said. "Water drips constantly into the room. At night, people scream in the parking lot below my window."

"I'd still like to come," I said.

"I'll throw you out," she said.

When I got to her room, I brought out a beer.

"Do you have a drinking problem?" she asked.

"Why?" I asked.

"Because I don't drink at all," she said.

"I don't think so," I said.

"Maybe you should go to a twelve-step meeting," she said. "The people there will give you unconditional love."

*

I went to rent a pornographic video. I walked down to a basement and looked at shelves of "slave" videocassette recorders copying tapes. I chatted with the bootleggers, browsed and took my pick.

I didn't have to pay for the video, because I had been such a frequent customer.

At home, I fast-forwarded through the tape. I planned to slow it to normal speed only when I saw a scene I liked. I looked for scenes of intense cruelty, played with a touch of humor. Unfortunately, the video contained nothing approaching what I was looking for, so I skimmed through it in about ten minutes.

Then I went back to the store, selected another title, brought it home, raced through it, and returned it. I went through this process repeatedly for an entire weekend.

*

The next time she came over, she yelled at me so loudly that a neighbor knocked on my door.

"Do you want me to call the police?" the neighbor asked.

"Yes," I said.

"No," my girlfriend said.

Later, I received a letter from my landlord that read, "We've heard complaints from your neighbors about noise. Please keep your personal problems to yourself or discuss them with a professional."

Soon after that, I lost my lease.

*

I found a new apartment that looked almost exactly like my old apartment, except that two-thirds of the square footage was missing.

Before I moved, I carried an upholstered chair out to the street. I left it on the sidewalk, next to my building. Later, I looked outside and saw that someone had set the chair on fire.

After the chair had been hosed down, it had a black crust, and yellow stuffing poked through its surface.

*

Months later, my former girlfriend left a telephone message for me. "I'm redecorating my apartment," she said. "Do you still have that chair you were going to throw out?"

I wanted to tell her what had happened. I wanted to let her know where I was living. I wanted to ask her what she was doing. But I didn't know if I would call her back immediately.

The longer I waited, I learned, the easier it was not to.

*

BACHELOR PAD

When I was ready to move to a new apartment, I called a man with a van. I asked him to bring another man, so I wouldn't have to carry my belongings myself. But the mover didn't bring a helper, so I had to work with him.

My old apartment was on the third floor. The mover didn't want to climb any stairs, so he waited on the sidewalk while I carried things down to him. I brought a mattress, a table, chairs, filing cabinets, electronic components and many boxes of books.

"Don't worry," the mover said. "When we get to your new place, I'll ask some homeless men to help. You can pay them ten dollars each."

At the new apartment, the mover walked around the block, looking for workers. He came back alone and said, "Nobody wants to do it."

"Then you'll have to help me," I said.

The mover walked away again and eventually found an alcoholic man who was willing to carry my belongings, but I had to pay him twelve dollars, not ten. Neither the mover nor the drinker wanted to climb stairs, so they carried my things into the entranceway and stacked them there. I took the items the rest of the way up to the fifth floor. The task took me until late into the night.

*

Shortly after I moved in, I needed to wash laundry. The building had a clothes washer and dryer, so I lugged a couple of pillowcases full of clothes down six flights to the basement. The last set of stairs was dark, as was the entire sub-ground area.

I switched on a light and saw a man on the floor. He was sleeping on a mattress next to the washer and dryer, and he had a couple of grocery bags next to him. I guessed the bags contained his possessions. The light woke him, and when he looked at me, I thought I recognized the person who'd helped carry my belongings into the building. Even so, I was startled. "What's happening?" I asked.

The man rose from his mattress and picked up his bags, then went up the stairs. Presumably, he left the building. I looked into the shadows of the large basement, wondering if I was alone.

*

I installed a lightbulb above a clothes shelf in my studio room. The bulb was bare, and I didn't notice that when I stacked my clothes, the fabric touched the bulb's surface. I turned on the light and left the apartment. When I returned, I smelled smoke. I saw a tenant running down the stairs, carrying a cat in a portable cage. "There's a fire in your apartment," she said.

I ran into my place, stepped to the clothes shelf and pulled a pair of jeans away from the exposed bulb. The incandescent filament had burned a hole in the denim.

I went outside and told the tenant that she could return, that the building was safe again.

*

One night, as I was leaving a poetry reading, a homeless poet I knew asked if he could stay at my place. "Just until tomorrow," he said.

He probably was remembering my previous place, which was large. I didn't tell him I had moved, but I said okay and led him to my new place. In my studio, we both had to sleep in the same room. I unrolled my mattress, and I gave him a foam mat.

When he removed his shoes, the smell was overwhelming. "When was the last time you took off your shoes?" I asked.

"Four days ago," he said, "before I got on a bus in Florida."

He smoked a bowl of marijuana and asked me which authors I was reading. I said Emily and Charlotte Brontë.

"A guy like you reading the Brontës?" he said. "I always thought you were gay."

He left before I woke. When he was gone, I looked carefully at his mat and at the floor. I was searching for small parasites, the kind that suck blood and cling to human hair. I didn't want to be picking any nits in the near future.

*

I prepared to leave my apartment. I made sure nothing was in contact with a burning bulb. I unplugged all of the extension cords to reduce the possibility of an electrical fire. I checked the window latches to see if they were shut and locked.

Outside the door, I turned each key a few times and tested the knob for firmness. I unlocked the door, came back in and pried at the window frames with my fingertips. I scanned the room for flaws.

I left again, turned each key a few more times, and wondered what would happen if someone came in while I was gone. Would that person unearth anything embarrassing? What if I got hit by a car and never returned? Did I have anything resembling a living will?

*

I walked down the stairs to the subway. The platform wasn't crowded, but I passed a few people as I walked. As I came to the bottom of the stairs, I approached two girls who seemed to be teenagers. I was going to walk around them, but they stood in front of me, as if they wanted to say something. One of them pointed to the other and said, "She wants to give you a pipe job."

The one who was indicated didn't say anything. I didn't say anything, either, but I wondered what a pipe job was. I could easily guess. I knew the girls weren't making a real offer, but I was interested in their proposal. The problem was, they walked away after the one had blurted her statement, and I didn't chase after them.

*

On my way home, I walked beneath the large trees that lined my block. The trees provided cover for prostitutes who stood on the sidewalks. These sidewalk standers sometimes stepped into the gardens next to the stoops, presumably to make deals or to dose up on drugs. Then they would re-emerge and flag down passing cars.

I generally ignored the sex workers, but on this day I decided to say hello. I walked up to one of them and said, "I've seen you here before."

"I've seen you, too," she said.

"I live on the block," I said.

"I don't make house calls," she said.

I got right to the point. "Do you do anything kinky?" I asked.

"No," she said.

"Oh," I said. "Sorry for asking."

*

I invited a woman over to my place. When she arrived, she said, "You know, when I got to your block, I noticed cars stopping in the street next to me. When I kept walking, they drove away. But one of the drivers asked me to get in."

She and I went up to the roof of my building. I brought with me some small fireworks on sticks, the kind you launch from a bottle. I thought shooting off the rockets would be entertaining. The tiny missiles flew a couple hundred feet over nearby rooftops before they exploded.

My woman friend discussed literary classics she'd read. She had an amazing memory for detail. She knew the names of the characters in *The Good Soldier*. She remembered the plotline of *Tender Is the Night*. I sat at the roof's edge and listened to her speak.

Back inside, I tried to tell her what I wanted to do. "I have experience," I said. "I won't hurt you. Look, I have a mattress."

"You might be able to do that with someone," she said, "if you got to know her very well. But it would take a long time before you got there."

We leaned against my rolled-up mattress and watched a recorded movie about a boy who was abnormally attached to his rocking horse. The boy believed that he gained power by riding the wooden toy. He thought that he could see the future, that he could forecast the outcomes of actual races. But he went too far eventually, kept riding the horse like a crazy boy, until he died in the miniature saddle.

*

RETREAT

Before I went away, people at my office made fun of my upcoming trip to an artists colony. They said things like "So, you're heading for a nudist colony."

One co-worker approached me and said, "I didn't know you were a nudist. What's it like? Do you have to be nude all the time, or can you wear clothes if you want? Aren't you afraid of getting sunburned on sensitive areas?"

Someone else asked, "What happens if you're just strolling around and you get aroused sexually? Do they allow photos there? Can you bring back some pictures?"

By the time I arrived at the artists colony, I expected everyone there to be totally naked.

*

At the retreat, I had a mattress in my bedroom and another mattress in my studio. The two beds, I understood, were for bouts of clinical depression. Whenever I felt suicidal, I wouldn't be far from a place where I could sleep off my despair.

Of course, I could also use my desk chair, a belt, and a plant hook in the ceiling to hang myself instead.

*

One of the residents had to leave the compound early because she was bitten by a tick. She said she didn't know if the parasite was a deer tick, a dog tick or a people tick, or even if the tick's saliva was contagious, but she couldn't stay in a place where she might be infected by a spirochete.

*

Another colleague, a composer, liked to vacuum objects with his mouth. He would suck up pieces of paper and cardboard— magazines and sheet music—by making an O shape with his lips and inhaling forcefully. He was so talented he could levitate a

Ping-Pong paddle without using his hands. I noticed he would usually suck things while people were talking to him.

*

Another colonist suggested designating a quiet table during breakfast—a table where there would be no talking, where people could contemplate their activity for the coming day. The man who sucked things said that was okay, as long as there was also a loud table, where people could raise hell first thing in the morning.

I ate at the loud table, where I watched the sucking man vacuum objects, like his napkin and his place mat, with his kisser. Once, he Hoovered his coffee saucer.

*

During a meal, a grande dame asked my name, and when I told her, she said, "You should drop your Polish name and use a Chinese name."

"Like what?" I asked.

"Like Wong."

"What about my first name?"

"Thelonius is okay," she said.

"Who would I be, then?"

"Thelonius Wong," she said. "You look like a Wong, or a Fong. Try Thelonius King Kong."

*

One night, a woman asked me to go outside to watch a meteor shower. When I got to the spot, I saw a group of naked people in the local swimming pool. I'd finally found my nudist colony.

I took off my clothes and slipped into the water, but the humidity fogged my glasses immediately. I couldn't see any meteorites or even any bare *tuchuses*. I was aware, however, that everyone else was checking out my keister.

*

Later, the woman who'd asked me to watch meteors invited me to her studio. I sat on a metal stool in the middle of a large, mostly bare room while she poured whisky into glasses.

"Would you like to see what I'm working on?" she asked.

"Sure," I said.

She put a video tape into a player and turned on a monitor. I saw a figure drawn with black ink on the screen. The figure was animated, and began to cry tears that looked like big black dots. Two streams of tears squirted up from the figure's eyes and fell to the floor, like water from garden hoses. There was more than one character in the film, and all of them were crying.

"I don't know why everything I do is so sad," the artist said.

*

I went to my studio and lay down.

Outside, tree frogs were screaming. I looked at the window and saw a lizard's silhouette on the wire screen. I heard a clicking sound, glanced at the floor and made eye contact with a water bug larger than any insect I'd ever seen.

I saw a dead wasp pitched backward on its wing tips and stinger, a luna moth's wings with no body, and a crushed daddy longlegs. I remembered that I'd crushed the daddy longlegs myself.

An itsy-bitsy spider vibrated between a lamp and the wall, then curled into a ball when I fingered its filament. A pale, cellar-dwelling spider settled in the shadow of a rafter and waited for prey.

Moths flapped around the lamp bulb—I could hear their powdered wings beating. Three tree frogs decorated the door frame by clinging to the painted wood.

Outside, crickets chirped, birds beeped, and a lone Holstein heifer mooed for her herd.

*

The woman who'd invited me to her studio left the retreat. She didn't tell me where she was going. In fact, she didn't tell anyone. I noticed she was gone, but there was nothing I could do but wait.

When she came back a couple of days later, I asked her where she'd been.

She told me she'd had an encounter with the man who sucked things. "I was bizarrely attracted to him," she said, "but he was so mean. He inhaled objects all the time and told me I wasn't good enough for him."

"What did you do?" I asked.

"I broke down and cried. He told me that was typical creative behavior, but I was still mad at him. So I went to visit my mother. She bought me a blouse."

*

Before I left the colony, the man who sucked things gave me some advice. "Learn to play a bubble blower," he said, "or a rubber hose. As the music builds, colors will rise from the notes. The more notes you play, the more colors you'll see. You should play lots of notes."

*

When I got back to my office, one of my co-workers asked, "Did something happen to you there?"

"What do you mean?" I asked.

"When you left the office, you seemed okay. But all that nudity must have screwed you up. Did you get naked with somebody?"

"No," I said, "it wasn't that way. Every day, I sat down at my keyboard. I hit letters to make words; then I hit the Delete key and watched it erase everything. Then I typed some more. I rocked and rolled."

*

LOVE FOR SALE

I didn't feel hopeful during our first conversation, and if I had listened to my instincts, everything would have been fine. Instead, I accepted her invitation to call.

Strangely, she didn't get my phone message. Maybe one of her children erased it mistake. In any event, I should have taken that as a warning. But I didn't. No, what I did was, I told a mutual friend I had called, waited for the friend to deliver my new message, got a confirmation of receipt, and called again.

*

When I spoke to her, she told me she'd left a coat at an airport terminal and asked if I would go to see if the coat was still there.

The airport wasn't close to where I lived, so I took a shuttle bus to another borough, got off at the departure building, found the waiting area, and looked around. I scanned hundreds of bolted-together chairs, but saw no unattended articles of clothing.

I went to the lost-and-found desk and asked if anyone had returned a long, tan cloth coat, and an official brought out a winter garment. It looked nothing like what I had described.

When I told my new friend I couldn't find her coat, she said, "Maybe you'll buy me a new one."

*

She took me shopping for furs. First, we went to a department store, to a section that resembled a bank vault, except that the valuables in the steel-walled room were animal skins.

She selected a mink and put it on. We both stroked the fur and admired its softness. The price, I noticed, was what I would earn in half a year.

We looked at coats made from other species. The rabbit, beaver and chinchilla garments also felt fine, and their speckled, earthy colors were pleasing. The raccoon was patchy but luxurious.

"I don't think these are right," I said. I knew but couldn't say that there was no way I could pay for one of the coats.

Next, she took me to a fur trade show. We walked across a convention floor, navigating a labyrinth of furs on wheeled racks. She modeled several specimens for me.

When it became clear I was not going to buy her a fur, she borrowed an Eskimo-style parka from a friend of hers and wore it in place of the coat she'd left at the airport.

*

Whenever I visited her at her place, my main job was to wash the dishes. After dinner, I would get to work. I was fast, but careful. Once, there were some orange peels lying around, so I showed her son how to make a flare by pinching the rind and holding a lit match in front of the spray. He liked watching the miniature fireworks, but he didn't want to hold the matches himself. "I'm chicken," he said.

My other jobs at her place involved applying weather stripping to windows, changing lightbulbs, and carrying the younger child when she was too tired to walk.

*

For what seemed like a long while, she always wore some kind of clothing to bed—a nightgown or underwear. Even though I complained, she would not remove the prophylactic layer. As a result, we became skilled at frottage. I didn't realize at first that I was getting brush burns on my penis from all of that rubbing.

One night, I noticed that the fabric barrier was gone.

I wanted to say, "What gives? Aren't you worried about penetration? What about in utero fertilization? Aren't you afraid of HIV? How about STDs?" But I didn't say anything; I just jumped at my chance.

*

For our next shopping trip, she took me to pick out an engagement ring. We walked along a quaint street and looked into jewelry store windows. When she saw designs she liked, we stopped.

In one artisan's place, we found a number of appealing gold rings. She extended a finger and slipped on one with a sapphire, one with an emerald, one with a ruby. She liked the ruby best.

The problem was, no marriage proposal was being made.

*

We often argued about sex.

I would say, "If you let me do what I want, I'll give you something."

She would say, "If you buy me a sports car, you can do what you want for a week."

I would calculate the value of a sports car and compare it to what I would receive sexually in a week. It always seemed that I would be getting a bad deal.

*

One time, she took off her outerwear, then her middlewear, until all she had left was her underwear. She lay on my couch and stared at me. She rested one arm at her side and the other across her stomach. "You can take a picture," she said.

I fetched an instant camera and snapped some shots.

As the images became clear, I knew I was a lucky guy. If I were to show the photos to a male friend, he would no longer be my friend. He might pretend to be my pal, but what he would really want to do would be to contact the woman in the pictures, forget about me, and go out with her.

*

One evening, she called me. She said she'd found a dress she liked and wanted me to see it. I stopped what I was doing and followed her directions to a boutique. When I got there, she was standing in front of angled mirrors, wearing a mini-jumper made of black leather. I bought the sexwear for her on the spot.

*

The one time I got to do what I wanted, we were on a road trip with her daughter. I had to use a scarf or a bandana—all of my real paraphernalia was at home—and I had to be quiet, because the child was sleeping nearby.

When she found her hands fastened behind her, she whispered, "Why do I always meet men who are disturbed?"

I wanted to say, "I may be a frustrated kamikaze, but I'm not crazy." But I didn't, because I didn't want to wake the child. And amazingly, the child did not wake. Or maybe the child did wake, saw I was doing something incomprehensible to her mother, and was only pretending to sleep. Hell if I knew.

*

Things went downhill after that. Maybe I wanted her to behave more like a leather rebel, less like a chinchilla chick. Maybe she resented the fact that I never came through with the big purchases, that I was not, in fact, a rich man. In any event, she started dating other men.

When we split up for good, she kept the leather jumper I'd bought her. I remembered that it fit her like a glove. I imagined a new man bargaining with her over what he would have to give in order to do what he wanted while she was sheathed.

*

TASTING MENU

To meet people who shared my tastes, I made a reservation at an S/M restaurant.

For the occasion, I wore biker gloves and a leather wristband, along with my usual denim. The outfit apparently wasn't perverse enough, because the bouncer waved me away. When I argued, he threatened to toss me.

I went home and found clothing that was more extreme. I put on a five-finger band with metal spikes, a rubber vest and a Milliskin codpiece; then I returned. This time, I was allowed in.

When I entered the psychodrama bistro, I noticed that the hostess was unusually tall. When I looked more closely, I saw that she was standing on a man. In fact, she herself was a man. The man he/she was standing on was lying face-down behind the greeting podium, and he was staying perfectly still. The host/hostess asked if I wanted to stand on him for a while, but I declined.

I sat firmly at the bar and sternly ordered a drink.

I sipped from my glass while a woman in a leather dress climbed onto the stage and begged the other customers to buy a spanking from her. She stood in front of a Fascistic X-frame, extended her bare arms, and sent out a call for bared bottoms. "Come on!" she screamed. "Who's been bad? Who's having a birthday? Who's getting married? You all deserve to be smacked!"

No one responded. The diners concentrated on their paellas and bouillabaisses. A couple of them stepped outside, presumably to make cell phone calls. The dungeon doyenne stood patiently beside her Saint Andrew's cross. She looked like a cat of nine lives waiting to use her cat-o'-nine-tails.

Finally, the bouncer volunteered for a spanking. I cheered silently as he appeared in his Skivvies. I laughed quietly when he bent over. I clapped aloud after each careful cat swish.

After the whip skit, the bouncer became positively friendly. He accepted congratulations from the women at the bar; he even engaged *me* in conversation. When I asked where he'd been before the S/M bistro, he said, "Jail."

"Were you guilty?" I asked.

"Of course," he said. "I broke the law for years before I was caught. But all of my victims were willing."

The next thing I knew, the high priestess of the Saint Andrew's cross was standing next to me. "Let's do a show," she said.

"You don't understand," I said. "I'm a top man, a macho master, a cojones cowboy."

She grabbed my ear and twisted it. "You'll change your mind after a few drinks, pantywaist," she said.

She told the bartender to give me a glass of milk, straight. I nursed the drink and watched while the whip diva abducted a woman from a circle of people and led her to the hideous apparatus. The spank mistress strapped her subject to the triple-X frame and got to work while the woman's friends cheered. When the flog maven was finished, she hugged and kissed the birthday girl.

After my milk drink, I felt no more submissive than I had when I arrived. So I got up and headed for the exit. But before I got there, I felt the swat of a hard, flat object on my buttocks. I wheeled around and saw the cowhide princess running away, paddle in hand, laughing. "What did I tell you, Milquetoast?" she asked.

I wanted to strap her to her own cross and thrash her with her own quirt. I wanted to show her who was wearing the chaps and spurs. But I knew, from studying the S/M menu, that a baked-bottom dessert would cost me $50, so I couldn't afford revenge.

I promised myself that, the next time I visited, I would speak softly and carry a big bread stick.

*

WOMAN WITH BREAST

I was about to leave her apartment when she took off her shirt and wrapped something around one of her breasts. She used something like a belt or a scarf. Or maybe a string, or a key chain with a snap.

She lay back on her wood floor, lifted her shirt, and drew all attention in the room to her chest. See, I wasn't the only other person present. There was another man, a friend of ours, sitting nearby.

Anyway, she rolled up her shirt, grabbed the wrapping, and used it to define a soft circumference. Her effort didn't last long, though, because the circled area was basically conical, and no binding could grip it.

Even so, the other man freaked. He looked at her, then looked at me, then said, "I'm leaving."

"Don't do that," I said. "Stay and read us some more poetry."

We had been reading aloud from our journals, see, before our friend had gone shirtless.

The other man had read a poem referencing "a single turd of the albino sea bat." The woman had expressed a yearning for leather, in the form of a motorcycle jacket worn by a stockbroker.

My journal entry had gone like this: "I was sitting with some boys, and we decided to compare our 'things.' The boy next to me took his thing out first. It was much larger than mine, but there was something wrong with it. It looked more like a lobster tail than a regular thing."

Anyway, on his way out the door, the sea bat poet said to me, "She's not pointing her nipple at *me*."

"I see," I said.

I shook his hand good-bye. "I guess I'll stay," I said.

But I really wanted to leave. "I can't stay," I said to my host, the woman with the breast.

"Why not?" she asked.

"I can't say."

"What do you want me to do, take a shower?" she asked.

"No," I said.

We were sitting on opposite sides of her tiny room—she on her foldout couch, I on her computer chair. "Why aren't you a programmer?" she asked. "Asians are supposed to be mathematicians, or scientists."

"To me," I said, "your computer monitor is nothing more than a smooth stone in a clear river under a blank sky."

"I used to hang out with football players," she said. "Why am I spending time with you?"

"To hike and scrimmage?" I asked.

"Are you sure you're not autistic?" she asked. "I don't mean retarded, just mentally disabled. Lots of people who look and sound normal are actually impaired."

I picked up the wrapping she had used on her breast and grasped her wrist. Her forearm's pliancy, coupled with its convexity, sent a rush of enzymes to my brain. But instead of fainting, I began tying.

"Is this your idea of fun?" she asked.

I went a little dysfunctional with the wrapping. I calculated the length I needed for maximum security. I mapped the most efficacious topology. I engaged all of her extremities for radical strenuosity. Then I went back and double-checked my binding morphology.

"I have no thoughts, feelings or emotions," she said. "But you don't have to leave."

I ignored her nervously. I forgot about her unsuccessfully. I displayed affection intermittently. Later, I slept fitfully.

Morning light woke me. I left as soon as I could do so discreetly.

*

LONDON CALLING

I went alone to London for vacation. Once there, I didn't rush to a stage show or a museum or a department store. No, the first thing I did was try to buy pornography. But since porn was illegal in Britain, I had a hard time finding it.

I started by asking a newsstand clerk, "Can you tell me where to find adult material?"

"What do you mean?" he asked.

"I mean reviews of restraint," I said.

"This isn't America," he said.

When I persisted, he directed me to a small shop many blocks away. I crossed a bridge, walked past some monuments, and came to a storefront. Inside, there were some leather tchotchkes hanging on a wall. A few banned publications lay on a shelf. One of the magazines was called *Captured Colleens*. In it, a man was shown riding a chariot behind a team of women wearing feathered headdresses and nothing else. The man was the magazine's publisher. In a text statement, he asked readers to send money so he could defend himself against legal action.

I bought the magazine immediately.

"Where can I find videos?" I asked the cashier.

"On the other side of the river."

*

I took a train to the periphery of the city. But when I tried to leave the station, I had to "seek assistance," because my fare card didn't register.

At the given address, I found a store filled with leather- and rubberwear. There were some guidebooks on how to wear second skins, but no videos. When I inquired about the lack, the clerk said, "Actually, we have one novelty video."

He handed me a package called *The Mistress From the United States*. The movie featured the eponymous dominatrix. She was a maven of spank, a doyenne of domination, a diva of discipline. Her dungeon was an S/M restaurant.

"Why haven't I seen this film back home?" I asked.

"We're not in the United States," the clerk said.

"Where are we, then?" I asked.

"England."

*

Outside, the air was chilly, and all I had was a jacket. When I came to a surplus store, I went in for a warmer garment. I chose a wool covering and brought it to the counter. "That's called a donkey coat," the clerk told me.

I trotted outside and found that the trains had stopped running. I saw other people walking home. A couple of young men were giving each other piggyback rides in the middle of a cobblestone street. Wearing my donkey coat, I trudged a long way.

*

On another evening, I headed for a poetry reading. I walked past antiquated buildings to a high-rise development, then went into a cafeteria.

I was early, and the host was the only other person there. She and I eyed each other before I took a seat at a Formica-topped table.

There were several readers in the open portion, including a man who tap-danced while he played a saxophone. He said his name was Shoehorn. Other musical types also performed. One self-described social activist sang folk songs. A woman did a modern dance in a black angel outfit.

I signed up to read. When my turn came, I declaimed about wearing a lei and getting hit with a beer can, then going to look for the bloody idiot who threw it. To my surprise, I was asked to read again.

After the reading, the host asked if I wanted to go out for coffee.

"What about the featured reader?" I asked.

"He's all set," she said. "He has his chick."

"He has a girlfriend?" I asked.

"No, he got paid. I gave him his check."

She gave me a ride in her car to Soho. After she parked, we got out and walked.

We took seats next to a window in a café. Shortly, someone stopped on the sidewalk outside. He pulled a six-pointed star from beneath his shirt and held it up.

"He sees I'm Jewish," my companion said.

The man with the star pointed to his chest and stood outside the window, then walked away.

*

After the café closed, my new friend asked, "Is there anywhere we can go for a drink?"

"We could go to where I'm staying," I said.

I rode on the left side of the front seat as she drove. She took a winding route past columns, stone walls, domes and pediments.

When we got to my hotel, every public space was dark. "You can come to my room, if you want," I said.

In the room, there were two single beds, and we each took one. We talked for a while, but we didn't do anything, because we couldn't agree on what to do. We disagreed for a couple of hours, until I said I was lonely.

"Okay," she said. "What do you want to do?"

"Well," I said, "it's sort of like … a hogtie. Have you ever heard of that?"

"Of course I know what a *hag*tie is," she said. "But my mother doesn't even know I'm here."

"Oh," I said. "Forget it."

"No," she said, "go ahead."

I unlaced my sneakers so that I had two strings. I wrapped one around her wrists and the other around her ankles, then removed my waist belt for the cincher. "I'm leaving you *hag*tied," I said cheerfully, "while I take your car and drive on the wrong side."

"I'd rather you didn't," she said.

I thought better, then, of tooling, while my companion was *hag*tie-chilling.

*

In the morning, at her suggestion, we filled the bathtub and got in. We sat at opposite ends of the basin and faced each other. We talked to each other until I had to leave.

*

MEMORY BANK

I remembered starting kindergarten alone—my parents didn't take me. I didn't think anything was wrong with that, until I saw that I was the only kindergartner without parents.

I remembered that I was more embarrassed by the buttocks than any other body part. Specifically, my mother's buttocks, though I didn't know why.

I remembered telling my mother that my father had three penises. I was convinced I was right—I had seen the three appendages dangling at a rest stop—but my mother begged to differ with me.

I remembered that when I was about eight, some boys asked me to play softball. While I stood in the outfield, a player made up a song about me: "He's got a great big *kisser*, and he's got a great big *pisser*. He caught a largemouth *bass*, and he shoved it up his *ass*." I thought the song was hilarious, but when I repeated it at home, my father said I couldn't play with other children anymore.

I remembered that the chore I hated most was practicing my flute. Everyone, including the family dog, could hear my whistling. The dog would howl as I blew out études.

I remembered that our dog was treated well, except when it had to run from stones thrown by my father.

I remembered that my mother spoke with an accent, and I spoke the same way. I said "asspring" for "aspirin," "windowseal" for "windowsill," "bayg" for "bag," and "schweemps" for "shrimp." Sometimes, she would make up words, like "Chinese cabbage" for "bok choy." Later, in Chinese restaurants, no one knew what I was talking about.

I remembered that my father used the word "fuck" a lot, as in "You're fucking-A right" or "So-and-so is a fucking, money-grubbing, war-mongering, mud-wallowing, bourgeois bastard." He also liked the word "cocksucker." I didn't know why, but I suspected that his affinity had something to do with his time in the Army.

I remembered that, in the summer, my brother and sister and I had to go out with my father almost every day and hunt down small wild animals. Mostly, we settled for killing butterflies, but on occasion we captured snakes, turtles, newts, minnows and crayfish.

I remembered that my father liked other boys better than he liked me—I could tell because he wouldn't swear in front of them. But he liked the bottle better than he liked anyone.

I remembered that my father would complete school projects for me. He would build complicated pieces—a model of Stonehenge, a replica of the Globe Theatre—out of Masonite, balsa wood and plasticine, and he would decorate them with tempera paints. I would carry the sculptures to class in garbage bags.

I remembered that I liked to play with gunpowder. I would pack the grains into small bombs. Then I would light the explosive devices and throw them out my bedroom window.

I remembered that our family dog was once a hunting dog, but it turned gun-shy. Whenever we fired a shot in the woods, the dog would run home. If we were too far for the dog to make the trip on foot, it would wait by the car until we were ready to return.

I remembered that there were no blacks in my high school, and no Asians, aside from my dark-haired, Chinese-eyed siblings.

I remembered that I spent a lot of time in the silent presence of my brother and sister, because my father had told us that we could not leave our seats or speak.

I remembered that I had a stash of chains, locks, grommets and pulleys hidden in a corner of my bedroom. I never threw the hardware away. I didn't know who eventually found the apparatus or what that person thought of or did with it.

I remembered hearing a lecture about sex, given by a high-school football coach. He called us gentlemen and said that one day we would be exposed. When we were exposed, we would have to make a decision. Would we drink a beer and become the world's greatest lover? Or would we play things safe?

I remembered that when it was my turn to play Post Office, I ended up alone in a bedroom with the recipient of my sealed name. We didn't get very intimate, but when we came out of the room, everyone was giggling.

I remembered that, after I'd moved away, I would occasionally visit my parents. During those times, my father's favorite activity was taking me drinking at war veterans bars.

I remembered that my mother sounded excited when she told me about my father's terminal illness. She almost shouted when she described his condition. Later, she said she still talked to him, even though he was gone.

I remembered that, in my search for companionship, I always felt compelled to explain my preferences up front—a habit that did me no good.

I remembered that all I wanted to see was a facial expression that meant, "It's just you and me. I'm talking only to you, not to anyone else, and no one will hear what we say." But the object of my desire was always talking to many others who were just like me in their need.

*

ARRIVAL

I spent some years living alone. During that time, I thought hard about relationships. The difficulty was not that I was unable to make a commitment, that I forgot about holidays and other gift-giving occasions, that I didn't enjoy visiting friends and relatives, that I was incapable of caring for others, that I refused to consider the possibility of offspring, or that I practiced the love that dared not speak its name. No, the obstacle was that I was involved with things—I was devoted to objects—that my companions were not so interested in. They didn't understand the deep meaning of hardware.

So I was surprised when I met someone who said, when I mentioned my area of concentration, "I don't know much about that, but I can learn."

*

Once, I said to her, "Please don't give me any static."
She said, "Cling."
I asked, "What do you mean?"
She said, "I'll give you static cling."

*

We spent a year or so meeting in public places and visiting each other. Neither of us wanted to move into the other's apartment. A lack of momentum seemed to be holding us back. Eventually, however, a lack of money propelled us forward. So we found an apartment that rented for less than the sum of our individual payments.

She moved into the new place first, and I moved in a week later. The first night we were together, she hugged me and said, "You're stuck with me."

*

Often, before we went to bed, I would ask, "Who is it going to be? You or me?"

Sometimes she would say, "It's going to be no one," and I would drop the subject, unless I felt compelled to ask again. But if I asked again, nine times out of ten I would get the same reply, and that would be the end of our conversation.

Other times, she would say, "If it has to be someone, it'll be you," and I would say, "Okay."

But if she did to me what I wanted to do to her, I would end up complaining, asking how long it would be before she was finished and we could trade places. In response, she would say little or nothing, because she knew that if she ignored my whining, eventually I would get tired of moaning.

More often, I would decline her offer and say, "I'd rather do it to you."

Frequently, she would reply, "I don't know. Let me think about it."

I would try to be patient while she considered the matter. I would try to be cool. I would try to appear unconcerned. Sometimes I would even say, "Don't do me any favors." But other times I would just blurt out, "You know, I really want to do it to you."

More than fifty percent of the time, upon hearing my declaration, she would say, "Okay. Take your chance while you have it."

I would make a beeline for my sexware, and then I would get ropey with it. I would turn into a little Houdini. I would begin with a square knot, move on to a half hitch, then to a bowline or a lark's head. I would create loops and wraps. I would lose myself in circles and twists.

*

After we had lived together for a year or so, she told me she wanted to have a baby.

"How would you do that?" I asked.

"To do it, I would need your sperm," she said.

"Maybe you could use someone else's sperm," I suggested.

"But you would make a great dad!"

I didn't think I was ready for daddy-hood. But after some discussion, we agreed that we should proceed carefully, step by step. We understood that we should be fully prepared. That meant getting married first.

The conjugal planning process took another year or so, during which time we visited potential venues, met with prospective ceremony leaders, listened to uplifting musicians, chose our song (an Elvis tune), made a list of attendees, picked a flower expert, snapped up a photographer, designated a best man (who was actually a woman), drafted a cake design, tried on fancy clothes, sent out invitations, and wrote our personal vows.

And even though my surviving family members—my mother, brother and sister—brought with them their own preoccupations, and even though I lost my fancy clothes in a taxi while traveling to a wedding rehearsal, we went ahead and staged the event.

*

Once we were hitched, the topic of offspring became more immediate. But I wasn't sure if I wanted a new roommate who would clutch rattles and rings, suck on a feeding bottle, grab jewelry, paper and eyeglasses, and throw teethers and blocks around. I didn't know if I wanted a new blood relative who would blow raspberries through his or her lips, say "Dwit dwit dwit" repeatedly, and squeak, scream and cry. I didn't think I wanted to spend time preventing a tiny person from rolling off any raised surface that didn't have a fence around it.

I had to admit, however, that I might be charmed by a small human who could bounce, flap his or her arms, bob his or her head like a dashboard puppet's, and twist his or her toes and feet like rubber with the help of fingers and hands.

*

One night, at a music concert, I felt relaxed during the opening set—a tympanic presentation. And I remained calm during the first two songs of the headliner's set—droning numbers with electronic beats. But when the feature band's third song began, something my spouse said put me on edge. "Do you think the music is too loud for the fetus?" she asked.

Suddenly, the crash and roar took on a baffling importance. I imagined a small being shrinking from the tsunami of sound, cringing from the mix of snap and pop.

I asked, "Should we leave immediately?"

"Why?" my spouse asked.

"Because this music is dangerous to unborn living things!"

"No," she said. "The child might grow up to dance."

Afterward, though, I couldn't forget the wall of noise. I asked anyone who would listen, "Can rock concerts cause deafness in infants? Fetuses can hear, you know. Sound waves can travel through the abdominal wall and shock the proto-eardrums. Babies learn to fear the sounds of the world before they're born!"

When those people couldn't or wouldn't answer, I found books about pregnancy, turned to the indexes, and looked for entries like "rock," "noise," "pain," "hammer," "anvil," "cochlea" and "deafness," but found no such listings.

I located plenty of literature on fetal alcohol syndrome. But I could not understand why the experts were ignoring the existence of fetal decibel syndrome.

*

We mapped out a leisurely visit to a hotel-like birthing center. We thought we'd stroll the halls, maybe go out for dinner, while we tracked the crests and valleys of a gentle crescendo.

But when the moment of birth arrived, all heck broke loose. We didn't have a chance to listen to soothing tunes, lounge in a Jacuzzi or munch on snacks.

The fetal heartbeat registered weakly. Medical professionals and the merely curious arrived to watch. I stepped into a surgery suit, with plastic coverings for my shoes. I was ready to run to the OR, or even the ER.

Then the fetal heartbeat stabilized.

*

The birth of our daughter took place in traffic. There was no splashing or relaxing beforehand, only breathing and clenching on the mother's part and, on my part, massaging and coaching.

After the delivery, the mother and I ignored the baby momentarily so we could talk to well-wishers. Then I remembered:

I was supposed to record the baby's times of feeding, her frequency of excreting. I was supposed to bathe her and play with her, soothe her, read to her, provide for her, hold her, rock her, and throw her up in the air without dropping her.

And I had neglected my job.

Her fluttering tongue and thrashing limbs told me this.

*

She knew how to get attention, though she didn't know how to specify the kind of attention she wanted. She knew her mother and me, but she had more fun with her mother, because she and her mother could laugh together, and I was frequently a stick-in-the-mud. She would stare at my stickedness, until I burst out with her name and the question "What's happening?"

Then she would grin and cover her face with her hands.

*